circumnavigation

circumno

houghton mifflin company
boston   new york   1997

steve lattimore

vigation

For information about permission to reproduce selections from this book, write to Permissions, Houghton Mifflin Company, 215 Park Avenue South, New York, New York 10003.

Library of Congress Cataloging-in-Publication Data

Lattimore, Steve
    Circumnavigation / Steve Lattimore.
        p.   cm.
    ISBN 0-395-85407-5
    1. West (U.S.) — Social life and customs — Fiction.   I. Title.
PS3562.A778C57   1997   813'.54 — dc21   97-19955   CIP

Book design by Anne Chalmers; type is New Caledonia.

Printed in the United States of America

QUM 10 9 8 7 6 5 4 3 2 1

"Circumnavigation" first appeared in *American Short Fiction*. "Dogs" appeared in *CutBank* and was reprinted in *Fish Stories I*. "Answer Me This" appeared in *American Fiction*. "My Best Day Was the Third Grade" appeared in *Sequoia: Stanford Literary Magazine*. "Jarheads" appeared in *Mississippi Review*. "Family Sports" first appeared in *Phoebe* and was reprinted in *Fish Stories I*.

To Madeline, born September 12, 1996,
and to Marni, for being in the right state when she was.

And to my grandparents Ned and Judy Moore,
without whom I would be much less than what I am,
whatever that is.

acknowledgments

The following people have made this book, and the stories in it, possible: Phyllis Gibson, Melissa Wescoat, Tracy Wilson, super-agent and friend Noah Lukeman, and, most of all, Susan.

contents

circumnavigation

THE FRONT OF the house is mostly glass, so from my chair at the kitchen table I see the truck before I hear it crunch up the gravel driveway. I see the man in crisp, clean coveralls, fresh as ice, the tiny body he pulls from the truck and stands on two legs and pushes up the porch steps. I see Lockjaw Watkiss, come to collect, a heavy knuckle raised to rap at the glass pane. And he sees me.

Lockjaw Watkiss is a strapping hillbilly I owe money, sixty bucks or so, from the time he yanked a radiator from one of his rusted junkers — something long and gray and humped — and rigged it to work in my old Datsun. That was about a year ago. Maybe two.

When I open the door, Lockjaw says, "I need you to watch my kid for a while. I got to drive up to Oregon and cut a guy in half." He takes a roll of bills from his pocket, snaps off a dozen or so, and hands them to me. A small face studies me from between his legs.

Lockjaw turns to leave, but halfway down the porch steps he notices the Pontiac parked at the side of the house. "How's that old car of yours running?" he says. "Toyota, was it?"

"Datsun," I say. "Not too good. It's at the bottom of a lake."

Lockjaw nods, strokes his long brown beard, stiff as snow. "That drop-off into the lake behind Jack Stone's Tavern?" he asks.

"Yeah."

Lockjaw scratches himself, nods again. "I know it," he says. He opens his truck door, lingers for a minute, half in, half out, says, "There's a helicopter in that lake, you know."

"No kidding."

"Me and the boy used to go look at it sometimes. You can see it when the water's low."

I nod, smile. "Something," I say.

When Lockjaw leaves, I go inside and find his boy standing beneath the ceiling fan in the living room, staring up. For several minutes I watch him watch the fan. "Are you hot?" I ask him.

He doesn't say anything, just stands there looking at the fan. "Hey," I say. He glances at me, pushes a chair over to the air conditioner in the window. He climbs up and puts his face to the vent. He points to it, says, "There's a fan in there."

"It's busted," I say.

"Do you have any more fans?"

"What do you want with fans?" I say. "How about some television?" Then I remember the TV doesn't work, hasn't since I got it back from hock.

The boy gets down off the chair. "Where are the fans?" he asks.

I take him into the bedroom and show him the ceiling fan there. It's turning slowly, barely moving. Each blade is bearded with dust. "Make it go faster," the boy says. I stand on the bed and pull the chain. The fan picks up speed until my hair is being fairly blown.

"Faster."

I tug the chain again. The fan shakes like it's about to jump off of its mount. Two more tugs and the blades slow to their original lope, dust beards intact.

"Make it go backwards," the boy says.

"It doesn't go backwards," I say.

"Yes it does," he says. "That switch right there."

I put my finger on a black toggle on the bottom. "This?"

"That makes it go backwards," he says.

I slide the switch up. The fan slows and slows and — goddamn, there it goes, the other way.

"That makes the hot air come down," the boy says.

"Do I want it to come down?" I ask. "It's over a hundred degrees. I think it's pretty well down already."

"It's for when it's cold," the boy says. "Not for now."

I sit at the kitchen table and listen as the hot afternoon ticks away. The dry grass hums, bugs snap in the heavy air. The mountain's nervous. Fires have been popping up like jack-in-the-boxes all over. Last week I was at Jack Stone's Tavern and nearly everyone there had a fire story — a woodshed gone up, a few acres scorched — *poof* — just like that. I kept quiet. The tavern is usually full of firemen because the volunteer department keeps its engine in Jack Stone's barn, just across a gravel lot. I haven't cut the weeds back from around my house or cleared away dead timber or tilled the dry grass around the storage shed for years, not since I quit work altogether, and I don't care to see the reaction this would rouse in a room full of firemen. Jack Stone's is the only place on the mountain for a drink or human company, and I plan to go back there.

I listen to theories about how the fires are starting. Heat lightning. Someone's flying around in a defective plane that's shooting sparks. Maybe the pilot flicks his cigarette butts out the window. It's all bunk, though. I used to fly, and I know planes can no more shoot sparks than they can swim the English Channel. Anyway, the only planes I see these days are Forest Service tankers on their way to this conflagration or that. Some days the sky's choked with them.

Around nightfall it occurs to me I should fix a full-on meal. It's been a long time since I've thought about such a thing, since Magda moved out. Before that, even.

There's no kid food in the house, so I get down a can of beans and a pot. I'm standing at the stove looking at them when the boy comes in and points to the sticker over the light switch. "'Conserve Energy,'" he says. "What's that mean?"

"It's just something my mom put there," I say. "She doesn't like utility companies. Didn't."

He reads it aloud once more. "'Conserve Energy.' It has to mean *something*."

"How old are you?" I ask.

"Five."

"Are all five-year-olds like you?"

"What does it mean?" he asks.

"Well, I guess you know what electricity is."

"No."

"Electricity. You know — power."

The boy waits, mouth gaping. He's awfully small, hardly a chin to speak of, nose little more than a nub. He looks unfinished somehow, like he needs more womb time.

I put the pot and the beans down and grab a wire coat hanger and take him out to the Pontiac, which Magda bought for me after I sank the Datsun. I pop the hood and stand the boy up on the bumper. I untwist the hanger and take my shirt off and bunch it up around the bent wire. "This is electricity," I say. I touch one end of it to the negative terminal of the battery. I turn my face away, brush the positive terminal with the other end of the wire. Nothing. I press the wire full on to the metal post. Scratch it around. Fuck.

"Sorry," I say. "No electricity, I guess."

I put the boy down, let the hood drop shut, chuck the wad of T-shirt and wire into the car through the window. We go back inside and I put the beans in the pot and turn the fire up under them. After a minute or so I hear a chafing sound on the living room rug, feel the boy's footsteps behind me. A static zap shoots up my bare back. I turn around and he's standing there with his finger out, smiling. "Is that electricity?" he asks.

The shock still fresh on my skin, I say, "Yeah, Goddamnit. That's it. Now sit down and eat some beans."

He climbs onto a chair at the table. I scoop beans onto two plates and we sit and eat. After a few bites, he starts staring again at the wall switch. His mouth falls slowly open like a baby bird waiting for some worm.

"What does 'conserve' mean?" he asks.

The subliminal hiss of the TV wakes me in the middle of the night. In the living room I find the boy on the couch, lying on his back with his arms crossed over his chest the way movie Draculas sleep in their coffins. I lift his foot and drop it. "Hey." I take it again and shake until his eyes snap open. What a thing to see, not at all how you'd picture a kid waking up. No face-rubbing or squirming around, just these dark little eyes waiting for an explanation.

"Did you fix the TV?" I ask.

He looks over at the TV, then up at me. "I turned it on," he says.

"But it doesn't work. At least it didn't before."

He closes his eyes. His chest rises and falls, rises and falls. "I just pulled the knob," he says.

I shut the TV off and go back to my bed, which smells vaguely of Magda, my ex. She comes around a few times a month to write out checks, for the power bill and such. She works at a bank down in Mariposa, manages the office. She has an apartment there. When she comes she sleeps over, I don't ask questions. I understand about needing someone. Anyone. I don't make demands. She keeps giving me money, I don't ask why. It's not that I'm afraid she'll stop, it's just the way things have always been between us. Unspoken, understood. We know each other's contours, each other's rhythms. She just got sick of mine.

The boy's staring into the doghouse when I get up. I stand at the window and watch. The doghouse is big enough that he could walk into it without stooping. It's as fine a one as you'll see, a shingled roof, knotty pine walls, my old dog's name burned into the wood above the door — C O R N. Corn was a Great Dane. I spent a lot of time both inside and on top of his house as a kid. I'd go there whenever I wanted to punish my mom for working so much and leaving me alone. I've slept nights in Corn's house.

This kid, though, he just stands there looking inside, his face empty.

When I open the door to tell him it's okay to go in, play dogs, I hear the hiss of the rattler. I grab the .22 off the rack and hustle barefoot out to where he's standing. "Better get back," I tell him. He doesn't move, though, so I pick him up and set him down a few feet away.

"You sleep too much," he says.

I crouch down in front of the doghouse and point the gun. The snake goes crazy, writhing and striking at air. "Not *too* much," I say. I empty the rifle — eleven shots — into Corn's house, every one of them a miss. I could go up and reload but I'll never hit it clean enough to kill it. So instead I lift the sheet of plywood that lies in front of the tall arching door and press it flat over the opening. "Here, kid, hold this," I say.

"My name's Jamie," he says. He steps forward, puts a hand up against the board. The snake strikes it — *thump thump.*

"Can you hold it?" I ask.

Jamie nods, and I go up to the house for a hammer and nails.

The ceiling fans run twenty-four hours a day now. Every time Jamie comes into the house he goes from room to room and checks each one. Sometimes it's quick — a head in the door, then back out. Other times he'll stop at one and watch for hours. A few nights ago I had to interrupt a session in my bedroom so I could turn the light off and sleep. It was past midnight and he'd been sitting on the edge of the bed, staring, since supper. It was just Rice-a-Roni, I can't see as that's anything to launch a stupor.

Magda shows up in the middle of the day, so it must be the weekend. She opens the door, purse hanging from her wrist by the strap, drops onto the couch at my feet. She looks haggard, her big features wilting in the heat. "Do you have a beer?" she asks.

"Sorry."

She unzips her purse and finds a pen.

"Wait." I lead her into the small bedroom. Jamie's lying on the floor on his back, looking at the fan, his mouth open. "Whose is he?" Magda asks. Jamie's eyes shift in their sockets enough to take us in and quickly disregard us. "He's creepy," Magda says, then heads for the couch.

"I'm watching him," I say.

Jamie shuffles out to the living room while Magda's balancing her checkbook, an act of pure concentration for her. "My name's Jamie," he says to her.

"Good," she says. She shakes her pen. Her purse is on the floor beside her. Jamie picks it up, goes out to the porch with it. I should say something.

Soon Magda is shaking her pen again. She gives up and reaches down for another. "Where's my purse?" she asks.

I point, and she turns and sees Jamie through the glass door. He's sitting facing us, the contents of the purse spread out between his legs. He appears to be reading a paperback book. Magda jumps up and rushes outside, yanks the book from his hands and sweeps up her things from the floor. "What's *with* you?" she says to Jamie. She sits back on the couch and shoves the purse between her leg and the cushion. "And what's with *you*?" she says to me.

Now Jamie is beside her. "Can I have that book?" he asks.

"No," Magda says. "Go play with fire or something."

"What's 'amortize'?" Jamie asks.

"Who said anything about amortizing?" Magda asks.

"It's in there," Jamie says, pointing to the purse.

Magda takes the book from her purse, gives it to Jamie, says, "Show me."

Jamie opens the book. "'Chapter six,'" he reads. "'How to amortize, chart loan progress, and calculate depreciation.'" He looks up from the book. "'What's 'depreciation'?"

"What are you reading that for?" I ask Magda. She doesn't answer, but flips through the book. "Here," she says to Jamie. "Read this." Jamie does.

For the rest of the day, Jamie and Magda lie in my bed, Jamie reading aloud from books. I sit at the kitchen table and listen to fire reports on the scanner. They say the charred mountain looks like a patchwork quilt from the sky.

It's near dark when I go in and find Jamie and Magda asleep, his arm draped across her face. Suddenly she springs awake like a new mother, says she's going to fix dinner. She brushes past me to the kitchen, rifles the cupboards and drawers, says, "There's no food."

"There's *some* food," I say. I stand behind her and we inspect the cupboards together. "There's cranberry sauce, there's a box of hushpuppy mix, there's Ovaltine, there's —"

Magda slams the cupboard door, storms out, and drives off, comes back an hour later with a box of stuff from the Johnny Store down on the highway. "If I ever see that again," she says, pointing to the cupboard, "I'm going to be one flaming hot bitch."

"We eat," I say.

Magda showers after supper, says she's been busy but not what with. Jamie and I are on the couch looking at TV when she walks by wrapped in a towel, wet. "My mother was born in Oregon," Jamie says.

"Really?" I say. "They've got some dumb laws there."

"Is that lady my mother?" Jamie asks.

"I don't think so," I say.

Jamie turns back to the TV, no disappointment at all in his face. That's somehow sad, it seems.

"You can pretend she is if you want," I say.

"What do you mean?"

"Pretend," I say. "You know. Make believe. Use your imagination."

"I don't understand you."

"Like playing," I say.

Jamie scowls, gets up from his chair, and sits in the one by the window.

Magda stays the night, we make quick, sloppy love. When I get up the next day, there's a note on the table, along with checks for the electricity and the installment payment for having the well dug deeper. The note says only, "The tit's running dry!"

I have just over forty acres. It's one of the smaller properties on the hill, I think. Mom paid twelve grand for it back in 1960. I can picture her with some piled-up hairdo, cigarette ash a mile long, one eye slammed shut. "Three hundred an acre, huh? Alright, give me forty of 'em." She hadn't had me yet when she bought the place, but she was planning to, she told me later, so she had the house built big enough for just us two. She was afraid that if it was big enough to look inviting to a man, one would eventually end up here. She'd been at the mercy of violent, alcoholic men all her life, said she was through with them, with men altogether. As a hedge, she took the smaller bedroom. She said I could hang around as long as I was a kid, but when I started to act like a man I'd have to leave.

I like the house. It's got two bedrooms and a big kitchen and a living room with plate glass windows on three sides. If it was much bigger, I might feel obliged to work in order to take care of it, but it's not, it's small, so I can sit and look outside most of the time and feel fine about it. Mom worked twelve hours a day at a roadhouse that was dark and cramped and finished all over with rough-hewn wood. "It's like being a termite," she said. She decided her own house would have windows everywhere, the more the better. She wanted to come home and sit and drink her coffee and look out at what all she'd done it for, even if she couldn't see it for the dark. She hinted once or twice that if she'd had more money she might have added on another small bedroom, given me a brother or a sister. But when you've got a house to build and only *x* amount of dollars to do it with, square footage is a finite thing, and she wasn't going to give up her big kitchen just so I'd have someone to play with. I'd have to be happy with Corn.

I like the property, too. The way it sits on the tree line, we have old oaks and boulders and brown field grass at the front, and at the rear, where the hill gets steep, narrow-waisted pine trees stand as tall and green as they could be. Beneath them is honest-to-goodness forest floor, damp and dark and smelling like pitch from the needles that pad the ground. Just above the first sprinkling of pine trees is a pond, and on the near side of it a ridge rises up from the water like a man-made dam. If the ground wasn't so rocky, you could slide down on your butt right into the water. That's something I'm always doing in dreams.

Jamie and I are at the table making strawberry milk when Magda bangs in through the kitchen door with another box of groceries. She's been bringing them every few nights after work, faster than we can eat them. She brought up a battery for my car, new clothes for Jamie. Most nights she stays over, sometimes in my bed with me, sometimes with Jamie in his, or on the sofa by herself.

"You wait right there," she says to Jamie. She goes out and returns carrying a paper sack with handles. She holds it open in front of Jamie and squats down. "Guess what's in here."

"What?" I ask.

"Not you," she says. "It's a present for Jamie. Can you guess what it is, honey?"

Jamie shakes his head. Then he says, "A present."

Magda looks at me, says, "You have to ruin everything, don't you." She opens the bag wider. "Go ahead, sweetie." Jamie's not looking in the bag, but into Magda's blouse, which is hanging open some. When he leans forward and reaches, Magda leans forward too. Both the sack and her blouse open wider.

Jamie reaches into her blouse. "What are them?" he asks.

Magda jerks back, then laughs when she sees the angered look on Jamie's face. "It's okay, honey," she says. She laughs some more and Jamie looks even angrier. Then she says, "Those are boobies."

"What are they for?" Jamie asks.

"Well," Magda says, "if I ever have a baby — which it doesn't look like I will — that's where the milk to feed the baby will come from."

Jamie looks at Magda doubtfully. "Milk comes from the Johnny Store," he says.

"Mammals make the milk and then it goes to the Johnny Store," Magda says. "That's what makes them mammals."

"I thought mammals have live young," I say.

"What else would they have?" Magda says. "Dead young?"

"No, they'd lay eggs. Mammals give birth to live young instead of eggs."

"Are you sure?"

"I think so. Hell, I don't know, maybe it's lungs."

"Anyway," she says to Jamie, "people are mammals. You are and I am."

"Are you my mom now?" Jamie says.

Magda's face drains, her smile dropping like fruit into the sack. "Let's give you your present," she says. She takes a book from the sack and puts it on the table in front of Jamie. *How an Internal Combustion Engine Works.*

Jamie opens the book and turns a few pages. He stops at a cut-away illustration of an engine. A line connects each part of the engine to a chunk of text that tells its name and the function it serves.

"Can you read it?" Magda asks.

"Yes."

She watches him read for a minute. "When's your birthday?" she asks. He doesn't answer, just stares at the picture, so she raps her knuckles on the table in front of him. "Hey," she says. "When's your birthday?"

"I don't *know*," Jamie snaps.

"*Okay*," Magda says.

Jamie gets down from his chair and takes his book from the table. "My dad works on engines," he says. He goes off into the living room to read, his glass left nearly full with strawberry milk. I hold it high over the sink and slowly pour it out. "*I* spoil everything," I say.

The rest of the night is silent. When I sit beside Magda on the sofa, put my hand in her lap, she says nothing, does nothing, even after Jamie's asleep. I go outside and listen to the mountain cool. The ground seems to glow from its earlier heat.

Lockjaw Watkiss repaired my Datsun under a sheet of corrugated tin nailed between two pine trees. It took him a full day. I sat on a footstool about twenty feet away — not for any reason except that's where he put it — and waited. His trailer was a short distance up the driveway. Behind it, acres and acres of old dead cars covered the piebald hillside. I went around to the back of the trailer every little while to drink from the hose, and each time a small, serious face appeared in the window. It didn't say anything, or even move. Once I went up close to the screen and said, "You stink," but the face didn't flinch, didn't crack a grin or disappear or tell me to go scratch my ass, so I just went on back to my stool.

When my car was fixed, I tried to pay Lockjaw Watkiss with a credit card. He looked at it, then at me. I squinted off into the distance, like there was something up the hill in the menagerie of cars that wasn't really there. Lockjaw wiped a chunk of sleep from one eye with a greasy thumb. "You can catch me later," he said.

I patted my pockets for effect. "You don't take Visa? I didn't see a sign."

Lockjaw looked left, then right. "There isn't one," he said. He handed me my keys and shuffled off to put away his tools.

Driving home, I flipped the charge card out the window as I crossed the Chowchilla River bridge. It was worth less than all Lockjaw's junk heaps put together.

Magda shows up again the next day. Though it's hours till nightfall, the sky is dark, the sun choked off from the smoke of a fire burning close by. I watch from the window as she sets the box of groceries on the porch, sits in the spring chair, and calls Jamie over to her. He climbs into her lap and she jostles him around, they laugh. After a minute, though, Jamie's through with that. He slides out of Magda's arms and walks away, scowling. Magda collects the box and comes inside, smiling briefly as she walks past me. She puts the box on the kitchen table, sits down, crosses her legs.

I wait a minute — not sure why — then go in and immediately start shelving the groceries. A *dot dot dot* sounds through the wall near the kitchen door. It's woodpeckers hiding their food in the wormholes of the rough wood siding.

"We need to talk," Magda says.

"I guess the birds figure the house will be here even if everything else burns down," I say.

"I need you back on your feet," she says.

I line up boxes of macaroni and cheese in the cupboard, talk with my back to her. "I'm on my feet," I say.

"You're not on your feet," she says. "You're on *my* feet. I'm still paying for everything. Food and the lights. Everything."

"No one's forcing you," I say.

"I know no one's forcing me," she says. "I know that."

I stop with the groceries, pour lukewarm coffee into two cups. I sit beside her and we drink. She looks out the window, brushes her foot over the floor like she's sweeping something away.

"I've done my bit making money," I say.

She looks at me, then out the window again.

"How much did I make that year?" I ask her.

"Twenty-six," she says.

"Twenty-seven. The book said, 'Make twenty-five thousand taking pictures,' and I made twenty-seven."

"I don't think making money is the kind of thing you can say you've done once and then that's it."

"I *have* done it."

"But it doesn't stay with you," Magda says. "You don't get to keep taking credit for it when the money's gone."

I get up from the table and pour my coffee into the sink. I fill the cup with water and drink that. "I have the house," I say. "That's all I need."

Magda sighs, looks out the window. "I got a new job," she says. "At the *Advance-Press*. I'm managing the office and the accounts there and doing some other stuff. I'm making more money."

"Since when?" I ask. "I didn't know you were looking for a new job."

"Since April," she says. "And I wasn't. There's more to it than that."

"April," I say.

Magda nods.

"That's four months," I say.

"I didn't tell you because I'm seeing a man I work with. Work for, actually. Russ Jones. It was too soon to tell you."

"Seeing," I say.

"Seeing," she says. "Seeing? You know? As in fucking?"

"Russ Jones," I say. "You're seeing Russ Jones."

"Yeah. Russ Jones."

I shove the groceries aside and hop up onto the counter next to the sink. I used to sit here while my mom cooked. I sat here and she talked to me and I talked to her. I miss talking to her, watching her cook. Our kitchen was always warm. Mom's voice, normally loud and gruff, seemed hushed in here. The bowl of butter sat on top of the gas stove and the pilot light kept it soft and ready to use. There was no room in my mom's house for cold butter.

"Russ Jones," I say.

"I want to help you get back on your feet," Magda says. "I want to, and I want you to let me. Then I have to leave. I mean really go. Okay?"

"Go," I tell her. "I'm on my feet." I slide down from the counter and land with a thud on the floor.

"I'm going to ask you to do something for me," she says. "Next week is my birthday —"

"I know when your birthday is," I say. Technically, this isn't a lie — I do know. I just don't know what today is.

"Just listen," she says. "Next week is my birthday, and I want a party, and I want to have it here. With you and Jamie. And I want Russ to come too. He's a part of my life and you're a part of my life and Jamie's a part of my life, and I want to spend this *one* day with everyone I love. And I want you to bake me a cake. I bought a mix. It's in there. I'd like you to make it and put my name on it and write *Love.* You can do that, can't you?"

"You want me to make a cake for you and write *Love* on it," I say. "Here. At my house."

"I know it's your house," she says, "but it was mine too for a long time, and even though I don't live here anymore, not really, it still feels like home, more than my apartment, and I'd like to have one last birthday here. Is that too much to ask, considering I keep you from having to sell it?"

"I wouldn't sell it," I say.

"Is it too much to ask?" she says. "Can't you do this one last thing for me?"

Actually, it sounds fair. She was here a long time, longer than anywhere she'd been before. She was a military brat, shy, slow on her feet. It took every bit of her strength to leave me and she's still not gone.

"I can do that," I say.

"We lead separate lives now," Magda says. "You know that. We have for a long time, even when we were still together. And I'm growing, in ways I couldn't before. Russ is helping me. He says, 'If you don't grow, you die.' I think that's true. You and I had dissimilar growth rates."

"'Dissimilar growth rates?'"

"Can you do this for me?" she asks. "Take this step forward with me?"

"Sure," I say. "Whatever is right."

I put the rest of the groceries away while Magda drinks her coffee. "Are you okay with everything?" she asks.

"Why wouldn't I be?"

"You know," she says. "Because we still fool around. We haven't actually stopped with everything. Not with *everything*."

"I have," I say.

"You have not."

"I *have*."

Magda looks at me, her eyes hopeful. "You have? *Really?*"

"Absolutely."

"Then can I tell you about him? About us, I mean. I mean, we haven't talked everything out. He and I, I mean. We haven't said, you're my boyfriend, you're my girlfriend, and all that. It's just something we know. It would be nice to be able to talk to you about it. I mean, we're friends too, right? Me and you?"

"Friends first, I'd say. The other stuff second. Maybe third."

"How third?" she says. "What could be second?"

"I don't know. Guardians, maybe."

"We've only been guardians for a couple of months. How can that be second already?"

"I said maybe."

"Let's say second," she says.

"Okay, fooling-around-people second, guardians third."

She gets up, moves in behind me, puts her arms around my stomach. "I know we'll still be great friends," she says. She presses her face into my back and squeezes. "You're the best. I'm going to help you get kick-started. We deserve more. Both of us."

I'm putting the Crisco in the cupboard above the oven, where it belongs, my arms over my head. Magda hugs me tighter, her breath soft and warm on my back.

"Hey, buddy," I say. "Pal. Chum. I can't hold my arms up forever."

The year I made money I had most of the elementary school business around Mariposa, from Ahwahnee on up to Yosemite. I had the dance studio and the karate school, the little leagues of both baseball and soccer. I did some industrial work for the milk processing plant down in Merced, some promotional stuff for the Golden Chain Theater in Oakhurst. I did the civic affairs stuff for the *Advance-Press.* Nearly all of it was humiliating. When there's a photographer around, everyone who thinks he knows best is out to prove it. "You should get a picture of this, get a picture of that." You smile, nod, say you already took the picture or you're out of film. People get offended anyway. By all appearances you're saying that what they think is valuable really isn't. For me, that's a hard thing to do.

Magda fixes supper — meat loaf and gravy — and gives Jamie and me huge servings. She sits with us and watches but doesn't eat. When we're through, she cleans the plates and forks and puts them away, wraps the leftovers in foil and puts them away too. Then she kisses Jamie's hair, rubs my shoulders, says she has to leave. She has a date with Russ.

I'm lying on the floor of my bedroom, my legs upright against the wall, feeling not exactly sick but not well either, when Jamie comes in and says, "What's the matter with you?" He reaches up and pulls my sock down, which is actually pulling it up.

"I'm not sure," I say. "I might throw up. What's the matter with *you*?"

"Nothing." He checks my sock again. It's still down. He runs his hand over it, pressing hard as if to secure it.

"You ever feel nervous?" I ask him.

"No."

"Not even a little sick at your belly, except it doesn't exactly hurt, it just feels wobbly?"

"No," he says. "Sometimes I get scared."

"Were you scared when your daddy left you here?"

"No."

"I would have been when I was five," I say. "I'd have screamed my face off."

"I saw you drink out of my daddy's hose," Jamie says. He grabs my shin and steps onto my stomach. For a second it feels like sick-time, but then he steps softly across my chest and middle and his weight smoothes down the bubbles.

"That doesn't mean anything," I say.

Jamie shrugs. "I wasn't scared," he says.

I push away from the wall and Jamie lies face-down on my legs, his head between my feet. I lift my legs and he's suspended horizontally above the floor. "Put your arms out," I say. "You're an airplane."

He holds out his arms, teeters a bit until I grab his ankles. I lift him higher and higher, make silly lip noises like a plane.

"You ever read the town newspaper?" I ask him. "The *Advance-Press*?"

"No."

"Well, that's where Magda works, and the guy who owns it is going to be here for her birthday party. How about that?"

"I don't know," Jamie says.

"It used to be a decent little paper," I say. "Nothing fancy, but good. I took some pictures for them the year I worked, of the new methane recovery plant and little league soccer and stuff. You ever play soccer?"

"No."

Suddenly my stomach muscles are burning from holding Jamie up. It's not just queasy now, it's hot too, and my legs drop to the floor. "Turbulence," I say.

"What's that?"

"Turbulence? That's when the plane hits a pothole. Anyway, this guy Russ Jones buys the paper, and you know what he does with it? This decent little paper?"

"No."

"He stops charging for it, gives it away for free. Only he doesn't just give it to anyone who wants it, he gives it to everyone, whether they want it or not. You know those papers you see all dried up in people's driveways and littering the roads in town? Those are them. Only he also quits printing anything people want to read. There's like two or three articles puffing up some business in town that buys big ads in the paper. No more Op-Ed page or sports articles — same person writes everything. The pictures look like mud."

"I don't know what to say about that," Jamie says.

"Nothing to say," I tell him. "It's a piece of shit."

I lift my legs high again and Jamie is soaring. "Make noises like an airplane," I tell him. "Are you a jet fighter or a 747?"

Jamie says nothing.

"Are you pretending you're an airplane?" I ask him.

"No."

"Why not?"

"I don't want to."

"Sure you do. Everybody wants to be an airplane."

"Put me down right now," Jamie says.

I lower my legs again and Jamie rolls off of me. "Whatever you say. No sense flying if you're not an airplane."

I started flying when I was in high school. There was a man, Butch Kelly, who used to drop his little helicopter into the parking lot of Mom's truck stop and spend the day drinking coffee with her and plunking Bix Beiderbecke tunes on his banjo. He never hit on her or asked for anything more than a refill, and Mom called him her friend. She didn't say that about many.

Butch operates a flying service out of the airport in Mariposa. He used to take me up with him in the afternoons, sometimes in his little chopper, which he called The Moth, sometimes in the Cessna. He let me start the Cessna by spinning the prop, and when I got interested in photography he gave me a multilens camera that had belonged to an aerial photographer who'd stiffed him on charter fees. On my own, I learned how to use the camera, how to set course and speed to area and altitude, how to make mosaics at a scale of 1:20,000 to cover many miles in one image, how to border a vertical shot with oblique shots from each side to form a continuous photo of an area, horizon to horizon. I developed the film at school. The photo teacher gave me free use of the dark-room in exchange for feeding his dogs on the weekends he drove down to Bishop to see his kids.

Russ and Magda show up for the party right at three. Magda warned me about Russ's punctuality; she thinks it's endearing, re-spectful. I watch from the living room window as Russ parks the car. The trunk lid pops up before they get out. When Russ sees the doghouse he stiffens, looks around. Magda laughs, tells him there's no dog to worry about. No Corn. They disappear behind the trunk lid for what seems a while, then it goes down and they're holding boxes. Russ looks regular — white shorts, brown T-shirt, a collar of russet hair around his tan, freckled head — and I get a little queasy thinking maybe I'll like him. But that goes away when I get a look at Magda in her shortie dress, red with bright yellow and blue flowers, sparkling like a drawer full of dimes. She puts a hand on his back as they head toward the house.

I met a man one night at Jack Stone's Tavern, a cowboy, hand-some I guess, with a drooping walrus mustache and big forearms. He said he'd come up here all the way from Bakersfield because he wanted to drive and think. For some reason he singled me out, kept talking to me. All that driving, he said. All that thinking. He compared the lines in the road to the days of the year. What could I do? I asked what all he'd thought about. "I can't tell you," he said. "It ain't right." Okay by me. I watched TV for a while, shot a game of pool. When I went into the bathroom, the guy followed me in. He stood behind me and stammered as I peed. "That stuff I said before? Well, what I want to say is this: Good and bad, ugly and pretty, they're right next to each other, you know? Not far apart like we think. Me, I never thought of my wife as beautiful, never thought of her any particular way. Then today I seen her with another man's dick in her and right away I thought, *Yes, of course, that's it exactly.*"

I grab the cake from the kitchen table, blow some of the flour from the sides of the pan, and meet them at the door with it. It says *Love.* There's a small chink in one corner that I tried to cover with frosting, but it melted and ran into the crack. Somehow that makes the *Love* stand out more.

When they hit the porch, I open the door and greet them, cake first. "Happy birthday," I say.

Magda beams at the cake, kisses me on the cheek. "Thank you," she says. "Really. Thank you." She holds out a pink box tied with string — a cake box. "I'm sorry," she says. "It's not to show you up or anything. It's for Jamie."

Magda steps back, takes Russ by the elbow, makes introductions. Russ shrugs, nods at the boxes in his arms. There are two, one the size of a computer, the other smaller, a cellular phone maybe. Then I look closely at them. The wrapping is black with $e=mc^2$ all over in shaky white letters. It's supposed to be a blackboard with chalk handwriting. Magda sets her cake box down on the spring chair and takes the gifts from Russ. He wipes his hand on his shorts and offers it to me. I take it, squeeze it, drop it.

To Magda, Russ says, "I hope my coming here isn't out of line." Magda shoots me a look, and I say, "No. Not at all." I take up his hand again, pump hard this time, smile. To Magda I say, "I baked you a cake."

"You must have known she was coming," Russ says. We all have a laugh. Then Russ says, "I know you two are just friends now, but this is awkward. No sense pretending it's not."

"Well," I say.

"Yeah," Russ says. "Well."

"It's just one afternoon," Magda says. "It's not like we're here for a *ménage*."

More laughs. Funny sound, *ménage*. I hold the door open and Russ and Magda take up their boxes again and head inside. She shoves aside the newspapers on the coffee table — copies of the *Advance-Press* I scavenged from driveways in town; the undersides are crisp from the sun — and sets down the pink box. I nod at the presents. "Looks like you made out," I say to Magda.

"I'm sorry," she says. "I just thought since we don't know when Jamie's birthday is, we'd celebrate it today too. He's never even had a birthday party, I'll bet."

"What about his real birthday?" I say.

"We don't know when it is. At least this way he'll have a day to celebrate."

"Yeah. *Your* day."

"Don't be petty," Magda says. She unties the string on the pink box and opens the lid. Painted in green and pink frosting over a sky-blue background is a ceiling fan, little wisps of white at the tip of each blade to show motion.

"It's something," I say.

"I wasn't trying to upstage you," Magda says. "I'm sorry if it seems like it. God, if I say I'm sorry one more time today I'm going to kill someone."

"It's okay," I say.

"Your cake looks good too," Russ says.

"Yeah," I say. "Maybe we'll eat this one and enter mine in the fair."

Magda gets us all beers, rounds Jamie up from his bedroom. She stands him in front of Russ, announces him. "This," she says, "is Jamie."

"Howdy, professor," Russ says. "How's the research going?"

"I don't know," Jamie says. He twists away from Magda but she finds his hand and leads him to the $e=mc^2$ boxes. He tries to fight her off but she holds him close and finally hugs him. "Stop fighting me," she says. "We're celebrating your birthday. These are for you."

"What are they?" Jamie asks.

"They're presents, silly," Magda says.

"I'm busy," he says.

Magda takes the smaller box, puts it in Jamie's hand. "Russ got this for you," she says. "If you don't take it he might cry. Do you want Russ to cry?" Magda looks over at Russ, half smiles. "He's not usually like this," she says to him.

Jamie takes the gift and sits with it on the floor. He opens it slowly, like he might have to put it back together the same way. When the paper rips, he looks up at Magda. "It's okay," she says. She rips the rest of it away and puts the box in Jamie's hand. It's a calculator. Jamie takes it out of the box and brings it to me. There's about a hundred buttons. He runs his fingers over them, looks up at me.

"Cool," I say.

"It's a scientific one," Russ says. "It'll perform every calculation a calculator can perform. If he takes care of it, he'll never need another one." Then Russ seems to realize he's talking to me instead of Jamie and looks away, embarrassed.

"Cool," Jamie says. He hands me the calculator and goes back to Magda, who's waiting for him on the floor with his other present. This time he grabs a corner of the paper and rips it away in three swipes. The picture on the box is of a towhead family cooling off beneath their new ceiling fan. Jamie rubs his hand over their faces.

Russ gets down on the floor and helps Jamie unbox the fan. He peels the cellophane from the blades, tears the hardware from the shrink-wrap. "You think you can figure all this out?" he asks Jamie.

"What do I do with it?" Jamie asks.

"That's up to you," Russ says. "Rather than having me tell you, why don't you just try to understand how it works. Think about it. Explore. See if you can figure out a way it could work more efficiently."

"He just learned what electricity is a few weeks ago," I say. Jamie grins when he hears this. He holds up his index finger like a magic wand and points at me, laughing. "Yeah," I say. "Ha ha ha."

Jamie stays inside with his fan when the rest of us head out back. I put out a little spread beneath the oak tree — snacks, beer in the ice chest. It's hot outside but not terrible, not so you feel like giving up.

I grab three fresh beers and we three adults stand over the cake that says *Love* and talk. Russ tells about the aggressive recycling program being implemented at the *Advance-Press*, which sounds like a canned answer to complaints about unwanted papers and trees needlessly butchered. Magda shows off, talking about amortization and devaluation and profit reclamation. Russ nods and smiles. I act bored, though really I'm impressed. The beer goes fast. When Magda shifts from balance sheets to politics and the free market — could Darwin take the Republican nomination? — Russ breaks off to use the bathroom. By the time he gets back, conversation has dropped to the level of what stinks worse, skunk or cow shit?

"That boy's tearing into that fan in there," Russ says. "He's got the instructions and wiring diagrams out. Man!"

"You think he can really make that stuff out?" Magda asks him.

"Sure," I say.

Magda checks with Russ. "I think so," Russ says. "I think he's a prodigy."

"God knows what genetic miracle allowed that to happen," Magda says.

"Kids can do things with their minds that adults can't," Russ says. "It's never too soon to get them thinking about the world's problems."

"His dad fit a radiator from a Model T to my Datsun," I say.

Magda and Russ laugh. "Yeah," Russ says. "Well. That's a little different, isn't it?" He goes to the ice chest and returns with a fresh beer. "There are special schools for kids like Jamie," he says. "He should be started pretty soon on a program."

Magda looks at me as if Russ had asked a question.

"We play dominoes," I say.

"There are tests that determine aptitudes," Russ says. "That might not be out of line at this point."

"Actually, we just line 'em up and tip 'em over. The attraction of the game itself is beyond me."

"So you haven't thought about his schooling, then?" Russ says, this back and forth glance thing going with Magda.

"It's not up to me," I say.

Russ looks confused. "But I understand . . ."

Magda looks at the ground, shrugs. "Lockjaw's not coming back," she says.

"You don't know what the hell you're talking about," I say.

I go inside to check on Jamie. He's in his room, fan parts spread out on the floor. I peek my head in. "So," I say. "Six years old. The big O-6. How does it feel?"

Jamie stands up, hands on his hips. "Fine," he says, shuts the door.

It's Magda's shot at the bathroom next. When she's gone, Russ says, "I don't know if you'd be interested, but I could use someone to take pictures for the paper. I've had to take them myself for the most part, but I barely know which end of the camera is the looking end and which is the pointing end. I just aim it and press the button. I know there's more to it than that, but I don't care to learn it."

"Not much more to it than that," I tell him. "Anyway, I don't take pictures anymore. I got tired of being asked to weddings."

"I know you don't," Russ says. "I know that." He waits a beat. Kicks a pebble. "But maybe you should."

"Maybe."

"I know it's not that exciting, mostly handshakes and mugs, but you've done it before, right? I mean, it's easy enough."

"It's still work though," I say.

"You know," Russ says, "I'll admit something here: I just don't understand that kind of attitude."

"It's more of an outlook than an attitude, really."

"Sitting around while the world spins by without you? That's some outlook."

"I'm not missing the world," I say. "I'm watching it. It doesn't need me to spin."

Russ shakes his head. "Is that what you're going to tell Jamie? That you contributed to society for a year but didn't like it?"

Right as I'm watching the sun jingle in the beads of sweat on Russ's head, a bird swoops down and pecks him hard on the skull, top dead center, then beats its wings in a flurry. Russ swings at the bird as it flies off. "Fucking bird! Goddamn bird!" He wipes his head, forces a smile. "What kind of bird was that anyway?" he says. "It dive-bombed me."

"I think it was a woodpecker," I say.

"It was brown," Russ says. "Woodpeckers are black and white."

"I know. With red head feathers. It was a pecker."

"It wasn't a woodpecker," Russ says. He chews his lip, looks toward the house. "Maybe that picture thing wasn't a good idea. It was Magda. She wanted me to ask."

I load each finger of my right hand with a black olive from the relish tray. "There's olives," I say. "Jumbos."

"I'm not hungry," Russ says. "Thanks." He looks at his wrist, sees he's not wearing a watch. He looks at the sky, at the house. "What the hell is she doing in there?" he says. Then he says, "Man, I'm drunk."

I head down to the house and through the window I see Magda holding Jamie on the couch, tightly, stroking his hair. Jamie looks absent, his body wooden in Magda's arms. I head down to the doghouse, poke a stick through a high knothole, jab it around until it hits meat. The snake nudges the stick and I scoop him up, lever him up to the rafters of Corn's house. Finally his lazy weight breaks the stick and he drops with a *thud*, hissing. I climb on top of the doghouse and sit straddling the roof, pretending to fly. Russ steps out onto the porch and calls down to me, "What are you doing?"

"Flying my pet snake," I say. Russ shakes his head, goes inside.

It's days later, a week maybe, before Magda shows up next. I boil hot dogs for supper, clean up after. Magda and Jamie sit at either end of the sofa and watch TV. I finish up in the kitchen then sit between them. Magda pushes me toward Jamie's end with her foot, says she's sleeping on the sofa tonight, or with Jamie. "Fine," I say. "Great. No problem."

We watch TV. After a while, Magda says, "I like television more now than I used to. Are the shows better or something?"

I don't answer. I have nothing to say to that. Sure, the shows are better, who knows?

"Let's go outside and tease the snake," I say to Jamie. He nods, goes outside.

"But we're watching this show," Magda says.

"He wants to go."

"I know," she says, "just —" She stops. "Fine," she says. "Go."

"What?"

"Nothing," she says. "We'll talk later."

Jamie pounds the doghouse with the hammer, stands listening to the snake rattle. He drops a rock through a knothole. "Let's fly," I say. I put Jamie up on the shingled roof and climb up behind him. "This doghouse is just begging for us to fly it somewhere."

"You can't fly a doghouse," Jamie says.

"Sure you can. Snoopy does it all the time."

"There's a rattlesnake in here," Jamie says.

"You can fly a doghouse with a snake in it," I say.

"No you can't," he says. "There's no fans on it to make it go. There's no wings."

"On a plane, fans are called propellers. Doghouses have inboard propellers so you can't see them. And you only need wings if you don't have a snake for power. We have a snake. Both are good."

"You can't fly this doghouse," Jamie says. "Quit saying that."

"Watch," I say. I bang on the doghouse and the *cashook cashook cashook* comes right up through the wood and the tarpaper shingles until the house feels energized, electric. The snake's lurching, coiling weight gives the house a shifting liquid center, like a giant, sloshing egg. "Here we go," I say.

Jamie stands and walks down the slant of the roof, jumps off. "I want to go back to that lady, now," he says. He bends down and says through a knothole, "You can't fly," then stomps off toward the house, pouting.

"Come back here," I say, but he keeps walking. "Jamie! Come back here!"

He turns around, says, "You're not my daddy, and neither is that snake."

You'd think it would take an audience of more than one five-year-old to make a grown man feel as dumb as I do now. But it's not just Jamie. It's me too, and Russ Jones. It's a talk with Magda hanging over my head. It doesn't seem fair, that. Small wonder we couldn't fly.

"I think Jamie should be with me," Magda says.

"He's my debt," I say.

"I can't come up here anymore," she says. "And I can't leave him here with just you."

"He was left before with just Lockjaw Watkiss."

"He's his father. You're nothing to him. Some guy who owed his dad money."

"Get out of my house," I say. "I appreciate all you've done, but you were right: It's time for you to leave."

I'm in the kitchen, listening to reports of the fire just over the hill, when I hear the muffled *throp throp* of a helicopter. I hurry out to the porch and find Jamie sitting there with his fan parts sprawled out. The blades are attached to the irons but the motor unit is out of its fake brass housing and the wires from it are in Jamie's hand. "You hear that noise?" I ask.

Jamie nods, mouth open. I take him by the hand and lead him up the driveway toward the pond. The copter is just visible through the pine trees — a whir of white paint and ghosted blades — and as we climb the damlike ridge, each step reveals more. It's got two rotors. The cab is long and thin. To its middle is attached a cable, and at the end of that is an enormous red trash can standing upright on the surface of the water, swallowing my pond. A fine mist rises like smoke off the water but quickly disappears in the dry air.

"I'm scared," Jamie says.

"There's nothing to be scared of," I tell him. "It's just a helicopter. In fact, I've been in that exact one. I took pictures from it of fire damage in Yosemite. You know what they're going to do with that water?"

Jamie shakes his head.

"They're going to fly it over to where the fire is and dump it right into the flames."

"Are we going to burn up?" Jamie says.

"They have a firebreak dug between here and there," I say. "We'll be okay."

Jamie holds my leg, his shoes against mine, his nose touching my thigh. "Is my daddy in that fire?"

"No," I say. "He's somewhere else. In Oregon."

"How do you know?"

"Grownups know things," I say.

Jamie looks up at me, suspicious, squinting from the flying dirt. "I want to see," he says. "Take me home." He walks off toward the house, the car, and I'm left watching this great red trash can fly off with my pond.

It's about eight miles to Lockjaw's place as the bird flies, twenty by these roundabout roads. The sky darkens as we get closer. "You want to drive?" I ask Jamie.

He shifts in his seat, grimacing. "I can't drive," he says.

"You can sit in my lap and steer. That's driving."

"I'm tired of you," he says.

"Today, you mean? Or in general?"

"Today."

"But in general I'm okay?"

"Yes."

"Is it okay staying with me?"

Jamie's permanent scowl deepens. He points up ahead and says, "Road closed."

A green Forest Service truck is parked crosswise in the right lane. An electric sign flashes from the roof: ROAD CLOSED . . . ROAD CLOSED.

I drive past it in the outbound lane, which is clear. Up ahead, the sun is a faint disk in the haze of ash. A car approaches, headlights on. It's a sheriff, his arm out the window for us to stop. It occurs to me that if I do, a whole series of things will happen, the last being that a social worker will show up at my door and drive off with Jamie. This may happen anyway, but not today. I turn the car around, wave back as if to say "Right-o, Roger, I gotcha."

When we get back to the house, Jamie camps out beneath the fan in the living room and stares at it with a vengeance. He won't talk, won't acknowledge me at all. I make an airplane of my hand and dive-bomb him. I tell him I'm the Red Baron, buzz his little nub chin and say *nyeeeow nyeeeow*. Does he even blink? I turn the TV on, flip through the three channels we get, turn it off. I go outside, kick back in Mom's spring chair and stare off toward the fire. It's a tinderbox of dry grass and chaparral between Lockjaw Watkiss's place and mine — what the firemen at Jack Stone's place would call a light snack.

After a while, Jamie comes out and says, "I want to fly."

"Fine, let's go warm up the doghouse," I say.

Jamie shakes his head. "In that helicopter. The one you took pictures in."

"That helicopter's working," I say. "It's fighting the fire."

"My daddy's burning up in that fire," Jamie says.

"Your daddy's fine," I say. "Your trailer's fine."

He stamps his foot hard, two times. "You said we could fly, so fly me there!"

A prodigy. How much can he really understand? It seems to me that if the map of his brain lays out like Russ and Magda say, those channels would be too deep and dark for a notion like abandonment to navigate. It seems to me.

"I can't," I tell him. "I'm sorry."

"I knew a snake couldn't make you fly," he says.

From the helicopter, the fire appears to trickle down Lockjaw's scrubby hill, through his field of cars, right up to the trailer. It creeps along slowly, like lava, almost flameless but for the yellow outline. The wind riffles down from the direction of my place, sweeping the smoke and flames to the south, where a much bigger blaze is tearing through the wooded canyon.

"Looks like you're gonna get lucky," Butch Kelly shouts over the pounding of the blades. "A different wind and we'd be looking at your place next."

When I called him, Butch let the phone ring about a hundred times before answering. The Forest Service would be looking for pilots and he wasn't interested. He was glad when it was me — there's good money in aerial photography — but then I told him what I wanted and he said he should have known better than to pick up the phone.

From my lap, Jamie watches, unmoved, as the fire overtakes his father's land.

"Should he be seeing this?" Butch asks.

"Probably not," I say. Then to Jamie I say, "See, your daddy's not here. He'd be out fixing cars if he was."

"Go closer," Jamie says.

"Too dangerous," Butch says. "Some of those junkers might still have gas in them."

Jamie strains forward to look up through the bubble at the blades thumping overhead. "You okay?" Butch asks him. Jamie doesn't answer, just watches the blades spin. "Creepy," Butch says.

What can I say? We are what we are.

"We have to cut out of here," Butch says. "It's getting too warm for my taste."

"There's my daddy," Jamie says quietly, almost a whisper. He points. "Over there."

"Where?" I ask, my stomach in a barrel roll. "You saw him?"

Jamie nods.

"His truck's not there," I say.

"I saw him," Jamie says.

Butch catches my eye, shakes his head.

Jamie shifts in my lap, leans into me. "He's okay," he says.

"We're outta here," Butch says. "Sorry." He points the copter toward home and we dip forward.

It seems like I should say something, something important, but nothing comes. I should talk about life, or growing up. Find a map and show him where Oregon is. I should explain the concept of truth, that his father's gone and likely won't be back. I should tell him that he can live with me if he wants, or with Magda and, eventually, Russ Jones. I should tell him about courts, how everything is ultimately up to them. And I should tell him that no court will ever let him live with me. The judge will think, like Magda does, like most anyone would, that that would be like one child raising another. I should tell Jamie some or all of this, whatever's the responsible thing, the thing Magda would think me unable to say.

But nothing comes.

"I told you he was okay," I say. "Grownups know things."

Jamie turns in my lap, narrows his eyes. "You're okay today," he says. I squeeze him a little, but he wriggles loose. "Stop that right now," he says.

On the way home, Butch checks out my pond. It's little more

than a wet spot now, flashes winking up here and there from the fresh mud.

"My daddy knows where there's a helicopter in the water," Jamie says.

Butch grins. "Everybody knows that," he says.

"Let's see it," I say.

Butch shrugs, heads across the mountain.

The lake behind Jack Stone's Tavern is low, but it's blue and clear. Butch dips over to the north shore about a hundred feet from the log-choked bank. It's like Lockjaw said. You can just make out the copter — its bubble a dim glow, a tiny thumbprint on the dark, glossy surface of the water.

"How come it's there?" Jamie asks.

"Yeah," I say to Butch. "How come?"

Butch cracks up. "Ha! You don't know?"

Jamie and I both shake our heads.

"I put it there," Butch says. He laughs, makes the tail of the copter wag like a dog's tail.

"What for?" Jamie asks.

"Yeah," I say. "What for?"

"What for?" Butch says. "Because I was drunk as an uncle, that's what for." He puffs up, smiles big as the sky. "Good thing I can swim drunk."

"Head over behind the tavern," I say. Butch leans into the stick and in seconds we're above my Datsun, another faint ghost beneath all this beautiful water. "I put that there," I tell Jamie. "You remember that car?"

"Yes."

"Your daddy fixed it for me," I say.

Jamie stares for a long time at the water beneath us, at the car, perhaps, or at the reflection of the helicopter's spinning blades. Then he says, "My daddy fixes things."

When Butch lands the copter in the driveway, I jump out and lift Jamie down after me. "Call me sometime when you don't want nothing," Butch says. "I'll fly up for coffee."

"How about now?"

"Naw," he says. "I got to go make money off this fire business somehow. Can't talk you back up with your camera, can I?"

"Sorry," I say. "I'm retired. Try strapping your old Brownie to a kite. That's what the old-timers did."

Butch laughs. "Retired my ass. God did all this damage for us, least you could do is take some pictures of it."

I shut the door and cover my face against the flying dirt, but Jamie just stands there looking up, too young or dumb or just too much a child to protect himself. I pull him close and stretch my shirttail over his face until Butch is gone and the debris settles.

We head up the hill, and when we get to the doghouse I ask Jamie if he wants to play with the snake.

"We have to let him out before he dies," he says.

"Yeah," I say, "I guess he's earned it. He's been a good snake." I pick up the hammer from the weeds and yank the nails one by one from the plywood board until it's just me holding it up. The storm of rattles rages on the other side. "Come here," I say to Jamie. I squat down, and he climbs onto my back.

"There should be a dog in there," he says.

"How about a Chinese water dog?" I say. "I hear they're smart."

"Dogs can't live in water," Jamie says. He says this, but he doesn't sound sure.

I let the board go and take off running, this odd little-boy weight on my shoulders. Jamie tightens his hold on my neck. His cheek bumps mine as we run, fast, then faster, finally taking the porch steps two at a time and stopping only when we see ourselves, man and boy, big as life in the glass door.

dogs

I WAS SENT HOME early from school for not letting Billy Pushkin drink water after I made him eat one stick of white chalk and one stick of yellow. The principal called my house and my mom's boyfriend said yeah, sure, send him home. I didn't want to go home though because Albert would be lying on the couch wearing baggy shorts and no underwear, drinking apple wine. I thought about going to The Liquor for a Big Hunk, but I'd spent all my money looking at Emily Klein's bare butt before school. So I went instead to see Blair Bodine, who was home sick. I'd tell Blair I'd started a club, charge him a quarter to join, then take his money to The Liquor and get my Big Hunk. Maybe check out Emily's tits tomorrow with the change.

Blair answered the door in pajama bottoms and no top. He said his mom wasn't home so I couldn't come in. In his driveway sat a red wagon with an empty wire cage on top of it. I asked Blair what the cage was for, but he wouldn't say. Then I told him I had an extra full nelson, did he want it? He said that he did.

Blair should have watched more wrestling. I pinned his arms behind him and dropped him to the mat that read *Please Wipe Your Feet* and he admitted he'd been playing dogs with the kid next door. It was a dog cage.

That sounds like fun, I said. Let's play. Blair said he didn't want to. I'll be a Doberman pinscher, I said. You're a poodle. Get in the cage.

Blair got in. I took the padlock that hung loose from the latch and clicked it shut. I'm not a poodle, though, Blair said. I'm a collie.

Okay, I said. You're a collie. Bark.

Blair barked. His nose was running and his back glistened with sweat.

You must be hot, I said. I wheeled Blair in his cage across the lawn to the faucet and squirted him with the hose. He whimpered for a minute, then I adjusted the nozzle and the spray changed from a mist to a stiff rope.

I'm sick! he screamed. Then, for no reason, he barked again. That was pretty funny, so I stopped squirting him. But then, seeing me laugh, *he* laughed too, and I didn't like that. I turned the nozzle again and drilled him. Forever.

Shut up, I said when he started screaming. Dogs like water. Especially collies.

But Blair wouldn't shut up. Cry, cry, cry. So I wheeled the wagon out to the sidewalk and charged kids getting out of school a dime each to squirt him. The hose was plenty long, and soon I had nearly a buck, a week's worth of Big Hunks. I turned the hose over to the kids with no money then and let them squirt Blair for free. I wasn't a mean kid, not like they said.

I was about to turn Blair loose — enough was enough — when a car drove by then stopped and backed up until it was in front of us. Four high schoolers got out. What do you think you're doing? one of them asked. I told him I was letting people squirt my friend for money. He took the hose from me and fiddled with the nozzle. I shrunk back, thinking he was going to squirt me, but then he went ahead and turned the stream on Blair. I didn't say anything about the dime. When he finished, he crimped the hose and offered it to another guy, a bigger one. The second one, though, said no, he had a better idea. He unzipped his fly.

Blair screamed like a sissy until the pee hit him, then he shut up. He crouched down and pressed both hands over his mouth. The sound the pee made on his back was a sad one, like he was hollow, not a real kid or even a dog, just a bag of garbage out in the rain.

Hey, I said. Don't do that. He's sick.

When he finished peeing, the big kid zipped up and they all got into the car. I picked up the hose, but the one who'd peed leaned out the window and said, If you wash him off, we're coming back for you. I dropped the hose and the nozzle clicked on the cement. Blair opened his eyes when he heard it, but then he said, It burns, it burns! and pressed his hands to his face.

I looked at the kid who'd peed and said, You owe me fifteen cents, you son of a bitch, tacking on a nickel for using pee instead of water. The kid didn't pay though, and they drove off, laughing.

Blair was crying so hard he couldn't tell me where the key to the lock was. Then a car that looked like his mom's station wagon turned the corner, and I ran. A long way down the street, the car passed me — it was no one I knew. But I was almost to our apartment by then, so I kept going. I was starting to feel sick too.

When I got home, Albert gave me a note for The Liquor and a stolen traveler's check from the wrinkled paper sack that was full of them. I walked to The Liquor and gave the guy the note and the check and he gave me three bottles of Albert's wine. Halfway home I remembered about the Big Hunk. I went back to The

Liquor and bought one, careful to use my own money, not Albert's, though I could have, easy.

My mom was home from her day job and getting ready for her night job when I got back. She said Blair's mom had run screaming toward her car as she drove by his house. She said she'd slammed on the brakes to keep from hitting her. What was wrong with me, my mom wanted to know. Why was I such a terrorist? Wasn't it enough for me to ruin her life? She smacked me on the neck with the cord from her curling iron. How long was I going to be a little bastard, she asked. Why hadn't she kept her goddamn pants on? She wept as she hit me. What was wrong with me, she asked again. With her? Why were we all like this?

I wriggled loose from her and she threw a bottle of tan makeup that hit me in the lip. Albert grabbed the sack of wine when my blood started dripping into it. First thing he did was fish out my Big Hunk, peel away the black and white wrapper, and take a bite.

That's mine, I said.

Albert looked at it real close, said he didn't see my name anywhere. He took another big bite, then ran his tongue down the length of it and threw it to me.

I sat on the floor in the corner by the TV and ate it without wiping it off. I stared at Albert and he stared at me. When I put the candy to my lips, the white nougat turned pink. It tastes better like this anyway, I said.

My mother retrieved her bottle of makeup and wiped it clean. She uncapped it and dabbed the liquid cover-up onto both cheeks, watching me as I ate. I saw from the way she looked at me that she was wondering what kind of person I was going to be. Strangely enough, I was thinking about that too. But unlike my mother, who four years later would leave me at Jerry's Coffee Shop in Hollister,

California, hand me twenty dollars and drive away, I never finished the thought. The image of Blair, pee-soaked and caged, sobbing, reared up before me and pushed everything else away. I saw Blair, and I saw the stream of pee pattering on his back, and I saw that it was mine.

I don't know, maybe the high school kids were real, maybe just a lie I told and told and came to believe. Twenty years later I can't say which. What I do remember, though, is the bitterness of that candy bar, the image of my friend, and the question that I asked myself as my mother stood there rubbing the brown batter into her face, hating me and becoming beautiful: *Why didn't you go back and let him out of that cage, you fool? He would have given anything.*

answer me this

THE APARTMENT is air conditioned all to hell when Russell gets home. His stomach clenches as the cold hits his sweaty skin. Norma, pregnant nine months, is flat on her back on the floor amidst a spray of sofa cushions. She's chewing her used-up crossword magazine into spit wads and launching them through a fat McDonald's straw at Hairball, their huge gray cat, who's hunched on the kitchen counter, hissing at the sag in the ceiling.

"What are you doing home?" Norma asks. "It's not even midnight."

Russell lies. "The press broke down," he says. "They had to change all the blankets so they sent us home."

"Oh." Norma grimaces, says, "You're going to be mad at me. I forgot to buy beer."

Russell is already mad, though. No beer just means it'll be longer till he feels better. He hangs his keys on a spindle that says KEYS, leafs through the mail — crap, crap, crap, a letter from the apartment manager. Russell fingers the envelope, knowing what's inside is going to upset him.

"That's okay," he says. Then he says, "I got the day shift. Till the baby comes."

"I thought management said no."

"They didn't say no. They said yes a month ago. I only found out tonight because Glenn says, 'What happened to you work-ing days?' I says, 'They never got back to me.' Glenn says, 'Well, they okayed it. The day-shift guy was supposed to tell you.' I says, 'Well, he didn't.' Glenn says, 'I guess he didn't want to work nights.'"

Russell doesn't tell what happened next, that he turned around and walked out, said he was leaving but not why.

"Sorry," Norma says. She shrugs, and the beads of her new cornrow hairdo *tic tic* like beetles. The hair is Norma's latest offen-sive in the battle to remain attractive throughout pregnancy.

Russell rips open the letter from the apartment complex. It says the water damage was Throc's fault, and Russell's ceiling will be repaired when either he or Throc pays for it.

Throc is Russell's upstairs neighbor. He's a good guy. Hmong. He farms a few acres of strawberries, has six or seven daughters, a dead wife, near-flaccid remnants of one leg, and a sparkling Chrys-ler New Yorker, a silver beauty usually found under the carport with Throc in it, just sitting there. For about a year now, Throc's been the target of pranksters. He came home several months ago to find his apartment flooded. Someone had broken in, plugged his drains, turned all the faucets on full blast, even wedged a plastic-wrapped bean and cheese burrito into the toilet and flushed. Be-fore that it was strawberry shoots planted in dark mulch in Throc's shoes, in his coat pockets and rice bowls, even in the egg cups of his refrigerator door. Throc transplanted the shoots into his own patch. "Good for me," he said.

Russell figures the jokers are Ag students from the college; the complex is full of them. They see Throc in his New Yorker and on Herndon Avenue selling his berries and get pissed off at the gov-ernment. During the Gulf War, a guy in the building across the way got bagged and beaten and rolled through pig shit for being an Iraqi. Fair enough, except he's from Venezuela and a nice guy. Russell doesn't have the heart to tell Throc it's the New Yorker.

Since the flood upstairs, the ceiling in the kitchen has been rotting, slowly caving in. A big rust-colored udder of pulpy ceiling stuff threatens to loose itself at any time. Hairball watches it night and day. He sleeps on the counter beneath it and every few minutes bolts awake, hissing. Sometimes Russell sees Norma lingering beneath the sag, sucking a Popsicle or just staring into space, and he gets the compulsion to leave, never come back. It's like when she turns the disposal on and hears it chinking up a spoon or a bottle cap and reaches for the drain opening instead of the switch. It wears a man down.

"I'm going for beer," Russell says.

"As soon as you walk out that door the baby'll come out," Norma says. "I can feel it."

"I'm just going to the 7-Eleven," Russell says.

"Mark my words," Norma says, straining to look back over her shoulder at the sunflower clock on the wall. "It's nine months at midnight."

"Nine months don't mean nine months to the minute," Russell says. "It's not a contract." He grabs his keys off the K E Y S spindle.

"So you're not going to mark my words?"

"I'll only be gone two minutes," Russell says. "I'll mark 'em when I get back."

"Promise?"

"Yeah."

Norma shoots him a face. "Grab my crossword for me first? It's in there." She points to the hospital bag. "Don't go through it, though."

Russell unzips the leatherette sack and dumps it out onto the sofa, a violent gesture he immediately regrets.

"Don't go *through* it," Norma insists.

"Christ on a cart horse."

"I said don't look!"

Romance novels, magazines, Game Boy cartridges, a lizard puppet.

"Quit *looking!*" Norma cries.

Cashew nuts. Gummi Worms. The Disc camera. Russell looks over at Norma. "A street map? What's that for?" He unfolds the map; the route to the hospital is highlighted. "It's over on Dakota, for crying out loud."

"We might forget when it comes time, 'cause of the pressure."

A Walkman. Her address book. Cheese and cracker snacks.

"Quit looking, Russell, damn it. It's not hurting you for me to pack up my hospital bag. It relaxes me."

Two cans of Pringles. Hair spray. Scotch tape. "You're bringing a thing of Scotch tape?" Russell says.

"Leave it a*lone.*"

"What are you going to do with Scotch tape?"

"Let it be, I said. You don't know how long I'll have to stay there."

"Your sister was only there a few hours."

"That was her fourth. This is my first. You don't know. Something could happen."

"And you're going to fix it with Scotch tape?"

Norma levels at Russell a chilly-eyed stare. "I could die, you know?"

Russell holds up a children's book, recognizes it at once as another insult from Hannah, Norma's mother. "'*Oh, The Places You'll*

Go!'" he says in a singsong. Hannah once asked Norma right in front of Russell how long she thought she could tread water with a rock tied to her leg. Maybe Hannah thought Russell's mind was occupied by the baked potato he was buttering. Russell looked up from his spud and said, "Longer than if she had one up her ass." Now when Hannah calls she greets Russell's hello with silence, and he hands the phone straight to Norma.

"It's not a crack about you," Norma says. "It just means the baby'll be special."

"I'm leaving," Russell says.

Norma's eyes soften. "Don't say it like that."

"I'm venturing forth," Russell says, "into yon night which doth have a twelve-pack calling unto me, 'Russell, I am your destiny. Belly up.'"

"Russell? What'll you do if I die in childbirth?"

"Almost made it," he says. "One foot out the door."

"I'm serious," Norma says. "What if the baby's sick or retarded or something? What if it costs a lot to make him well or I go blind having him and have to buy all special stuff for blind people and have someone stay here with me while you're at work?"

"Your crossword ain't here," Russell says. "I'll pick you up one."

Norma troops out the worried look, the one that says she didn't mean to ask such terrible questions even though she thinks about them all the time, as Russell does.

"Hush," Russell says. "Don't worry about that. It's cheap to be blind, anyway."

"You're coming right back, aren't you?" Norma asks.

"Oh, the places I'll go, Norma."

"Russell? Kiss me."

Russell comes back inside, lowers his face to Norma's but not all the way. She heaves her weight up from the cushions, a full-belly sit-up, and reaches for Russell with her mouth. He pulls back a little, and Norma's brow quivers from the strain. She lunges, and Russell moves just beyond her range, the tiniest bit. She gives up, lowers herself back to the floor and slides a cushion beneath her butt. "Forget it," she says. Russell leans down and kisses her fully and affectionately. He runs his fingers then his lips across her furrowed scalp. It's something he hoped never to see, his wife's scalp. Like the soft spot on a baby's head, it can mean nothing good. Norma and Russell talk a lot about soft spots.

"I'll tell Throc I'm home but I'm leaving," Russell says. Because Throc doesn't have a phone in his apartment (though he has one in his New Yorker), Russell melted a two-pound candle around one end of a mop handle so from the couch Norma can bang on the ceiling, Throc's floor, without having to stand. It's basically a big gong-beater. He puts it next to Norma on the floor, realizes it won't reach from there but says nothing. He's not even supposed to be home yet, for crying out loud. He starts out the door then stops, can't help himself. "Norma," he says, "Answer me this: You think people start life doomed and work their way loose, or vice versa?"

"You're just saying that to be mean," Norma says. "That kind of talk doesn't have anything to do with us and I'm not going to listen."

"I know," Russell says. "Never mind. Just bang on the ceiling if you need anything. But don't bang on the sag."

"I know not to bang on the sag."

"I'm just saying," Russell says.

"Well don't say."

"Fine. Bang on whatever you want to bang on."

"Don't be long," Norma says. "I can tell something's going to happen."

Russell is leaving the 7-Eleven parking lot when the car in front of him stops and blocks the exit. Russell guns his engine, honks, waits. He pictures Norma beached there on the floor, the too-short mop handle, the ceiling sag. He was wrong to scare her with philosophy stuff. When she hears that kind of talk, she thinks he's trying to figure out a way to leave her and feel okay about it. Maybe she'd be better off. Russell makes $6.25 an hour catching advertising inserts as they come inky and stinking off the Goss Community press. The conveyer belt feeds him tab after tab of Save Mart ads and Gottschalk's ads and Mervyn's ads and the motor's *whump whump* and the *tic tic tic* of the folder batter his brain with questions. Mostly he keeps them to himself.

"How about it?" Russell calls out the window. He inches the van forward and kisses the little car's bumper with his own — a peck, really. But the driver's door opens, and Russell knows it was a mistake. A husky boy-man with a dimpled chin and greasy ball cap, too stout for such a putt-putt car, strides slowly up to Russell's door. He's got mean eyes, and Russell knows he won't easily be turned away.

Russell flashes his palm. "Sorry," he says. "Foot slipped off the clutch."

The guy opens Russell's door, steps back. "C'mon," he says. "Me and you are gonna fight."

Russell rips a Bud from the twelve-pack on the seat next to him and offers it to the guy. "I'm not fighting anybody," Russell says. Then he says, "That's one of those old two-cylinder Honda cars, ain't it?"

"You're not going to talk your way out of it," the guy says.

"Friend," Russell says. "I'm not worth it." The guy backs up from Russell's door, beckons him down, balls his fat fists. Russell looks at the beer warming beside him, shakes his head. "Okay," he says. "Goddamnit."

As he steps down from the van, a ceramic *clack* chinks in his head, a solid nine-ball break. He feels it in his teeth a little but not much besides, realizes the guy has already landed a quick shot to his chin, not very hard.

"And don't call me friend," the guy says. "I'm 'bout to put a whomp on you."

For some reason, Russell's mind is calm as crystal, a moment of pure consciousness tinkling in his head. He sees himself from this guy's eyes, imagines how it might feel to drop a quick one onto the chin of a stranger in a buzzing, white-lit 7-Eleven parking lot in Fresno, California, at midnight, the most unnatural hour of a most unusual day. It occurs to Russell that if this guy would look at him the same way they wouldn't have to fight. Russell could go home and drink his beer and Norma would drop the baby spank on time, things would go as they should.

The *clack* of Russell's teeth has him in mind of the Chaffee Zoo, where Norma dragged him to celebrate being pregnant. Maybe he should tell this stranger about that, how he and Norma lingered on the bench by the reptile house, a wobbly happiness in the air, saying baby names out loud — Timothy, Thomas, Tad — when they heard a far-off *clack*, and were for a moment yanked from their reverie. They listened, asked questions with their eyes, then heard it again. "What the hell is that?" Russell asked Norma. She shrugged. They looked around, heard it again — *clack!* Finally Norma saw; she pointed out to Russell the huge tortoises stacked two high behind a bush, humping. It was a moment for Russell and Norma, who could say why? Russell described it on the drive home as a feeling of being suspended in some cosmic solution, not quite liquid or air, outer space maybe. A feeling that he was where he was supposed to be, a star in the constellation. Norma said she felt it too, but Russell already knew that she had. They kissed. Norma asked if a turtle would be an okay pet for the baby, what with the soft spot and all. Russell allowed that it would.

Russell notices the guy's belt buckle, his name in silver letters — *Doug*. "My wife's having a baby, Doug. Right now." He turns to mount the van and Doug knocks him a crashing blow to the ear that goes off like dynamite inside his head.

Russell wheels around, says, "*That* was uncalled for."

"Fight," Doug says.

Russell looks over at the nose of his van, still in midsmooch with Doug's bumper. He knows he's going to have to hit him, doesn't want to but what in the goddamn hell is a man expected to do? Circumstances arise, don't they? Things change.

Russell fires a stiff right, and the button of Doug's nose bursts like a ripe tomato. He doubles over, drops to one knee.

It's terrible to have a broken nose. The eyes flood instantly and a man can't see to defend himself. The palate feels like a hot coal. Whatever shirt you have on, that's ruined.

"See?" Russell says. "If you'd have just shown some courtesy to begin with."

A police car pulls into the lot, blue lights thrumming a note of cool-headed civic intervention. Most people Russell knows dislike the police, but not him. He drives right, with consideration and re-straint, and so doesn't get that sick feeling when he sees lights in his mirror.

Two cops get out, a man and woman. The woman is young, Russell's age. Loose strands of fine black hair dangle about her temples, the rest is pinned up beneath her hat. "Evening," he says to her. Without word or ceremony, she takes his arm and pins him face-forward against his van. "You don't have to worry about me," Russell says. "I'm calm."

"Shut your mouth," she says. She pats Russell down, turns him again and points to Doug, who's sitting Indian style on the ground, bleeding into his cupped palm. "You do this?"

"Not happily," Russell says.

"You want to go to jail?"

"No."

"Did you do it?"

"Yeah. But he blocked the exit, then drug me out of my van and hit me. Two times."

"He hit my car on purpose," Doug says.

It occurs to Russell that now would be the time to tell this woman about Norma, about the mop handle that won't reach the ceiling and the baby that damn sure will come at midnight if that's when Norma's of a mind to have it. But he doesn't. Instead, he says, "It's true. I gave him a little nudge."

The cop looks in the window of Russell's van, sees the twelve on the seat. "How much have you had to drink tonight?" she asks him.

"It was just a tap," Russell says. "To get him moving."

"To drink. How much?"

"Why ain't you asking him anything? I'm the victim."

"You're either going to tell me how much you've had to drink or you're going to jail. Choose."

"I haven't had nothing to drink," Russell says. "Zero! What is this, anyway? I was only upholding the law."

"Okay," the cop says, "maybe you're not drunk." She turns Russell around, cuffs him anyway. "But you are disorderly. And you're pissing me off."

Russell waits in the buzzing light, handcuffed. A police van pulls up over the curb — the exit's *still* blocked — and the cop hands Russell over to its driver. He's tall, with pocked yellow skin and the tired, hangdog look of a man expecting the worst. "You going to give me any grief?" he asks Russell.

"I'm not even supposed to be here," Russell says.

The cop nods. "Uh-huh." He opens the police van's back door and conducts Russell inside, sits him on a plastic bench against one wall. A black man is slumped at the far end of the seat, asleep against the wire screen separating back from front. He's got on jeans and an American flag button-up shirt, socks but no shoes, and a narrow, white straw cowboy hat arched atop his head like a hissing cat. Kicked back on the bench across from Russell are two Mexican boys, can't be more than fourteen.

"Hola," Russell says to the boys.

The smaller of the kids shakes his head, turns to his buddy and says, "Hey man, hola."

The other kid laughs. "Hola, yeah. Hey, that's Mexican, ain't it? The boy's a home piece."

They all sit for a while, the kids laughing and nudging the black guy's feet. "Hola," they say to him. "Hey you! Hola." He doesn't stir.

The van door opens again, and Doug is shoved in across from Russell, a twist of Kleenex in each nostril. In his broken-nose voice he says to Russell, "What are you lookid ad, screwjack?"

"I didn't want to hit you," Russell says.

"Fuck you."

The police van drives around for a while, doesn't seem to be headed anywhere in particular. "What are they going to do with my van?" Russell asks the hangdog cop.

"Tow it," the cop says.

"That's going to cost something, ain't it?" Russell says.

"Sure is," the cop says.

Doug looks at the roof of the van, screws up his face and says, "I need a smoke!" He bangs his head three times hard against the wall, and his face empties. "Ow."

"That wasn't very smart," Russell says.

"There's no smoking," the cop says. "And shut up."

"I want to smoke," Doug moans. "Now!"

The cop stops the van, turns around in his seat. "How about if I come back there and kick the shit out of you instead," he says.

Doug dishes back an even stare. "Smoke," he says.

The black guy says, "Shut up, motherfuckers. Let a nigger sleep." The cop whacks the metal grill near the guy's head, puts the van in gear and drives.

Doug leans his head back again, blood draining down his throat probably, into his mouth, his stomach. Russell can taste it just looking at him.

"You got cigarettes?" Russell asks. Doug nods at his breast pocket. "Hold on," Russell says. He raises himself off the plastic bench, slips his cuffed hands beneath his ass, behind his legs, bends his knees tight and draws his feet through the hoop of his arms. Doug leans forward and Russell takes out the cigarettes, tosses a few that are soaked with blood and puts a clean one in Doug's mouth.

Doug smiles, thrusts his hip toward Russell, the front pocket of his pants, says, "Lighter."

"Shit," Russell says. He reaches into Doug's pocket with two fingers, finds the lighter, lights him.

"Have one," Doug says.

"Don't smoke," Russell says.

"C'mon," Doug says. "Smoke."

Russell takes out another cigarette, lights it, lets it dangle from his lip but doesn't suck.

A lazy grin spreads over Doug's face, his cigarette glowing in the dark van. "Ah."

As he sighs, the cigarette drops into his shirt front. He snaps forward, stands up and bangs his head on the roof, dances around. "Aaah! Aaah!" He tries to shrink himself in his shirt but the fabric is taut around his fat stomach. The van pulls over, the cop gets out. The overhead light buzzes on when the door opens. Doug's screaming. "Cigarette! Ow! Ow!" The cop slaps Doug's stomach until the cigarette must be smashed up in there. The filter falls out, tobacco sifts to the floor. The cop lifts Doug's shirt and a bright pink eyeball of a blister stares straight at Russell.

"Looks like a pork rind," the cop says. He turns to Russell, sees the cigarette in his mouth, his hands in his lap instead of behind him. Just like Moe from *The Three Stooges*, he says, "Wise guy, huh? Want to smoke?"

Russell says nothing. The black guy sits up, says, "Yo, smokes, man? Give a nigger a butt."

The cop slaps Doug's belly and pushes him back onto the bench. "Eat a salad once in a while," he says. He grabs Russell by the back of his neck and jerks him out of the van, slams him against the door. "On your knees," he says.

"I can't," Russell says. "The coating on the inside of my patellas is worn off from laying tile. I got bad kneecaps."

"I don't have time for you, funny boy," the cop says. He drills his foot into the back of Russell's leg and Russell goes down onto one knee in the gravelly street. The cop ratchets his knee into Russell's chest until he's on his back. He unlocks the cuffs, rolls Russell onto his stomach, and snaps the cuffs shut again behind his back, this time through his belt loop. Russell tries to move his arms but can't. The pavement is hot and gritty against his cheek.

"Are we going anywhere in particular?" Russell asks. "Or just cruising?"

"Don't worry about it," the cop says. He flicks Russell's ear with the tip of his shoe.

"My wife's having a baby," Russell says. "I'm not supposed to be here."

The cop stands over Russell, grips him by the forearms, and lifts until Russell is on his feet. He looks Russell up and down, says, "You really think that's smart?" He opens the van door, shoves Russell inside. "If I have to stop this van again," he says, "everyone gets a crack in the head."

When Russell is released at six A.M., Throc and Norma are in the jail waiting room.

"Hi," Throc says. He wriggles his finger at Russell, squints and grins. "We drive around looking for you. Woman at 7-Eleven say you arrested. Fighting, hi." He looks Russell over. "Good fighter, hi. Face look good. It's good."

"How was your beer?" Norma asks.

"I never had one," Russell says. "And I wasn't fighting. I was a victim."

Throc says, "Victim, hi? Aha. Aha. Okay."

"I called," Russell says. "There was no answer."

"We were probably in the car," Norma says. "It's got a phone, you know."

"I didn't know the number," Russell says. Then he says, "I thought you were having the baby. It's nine months."

"I was waiting for you," Norma says. "But I'm ready. I can have it any time I want."

"She waiting for you," Throc says. "She strong one, hi."

"Waiting for me?" Russell asks.

Norma nods, her beads *tic.*

The morning sky is pink and blue, baby colors. Throc's kids are all piled into the New Yorker, waiting for Russell. He climbs into the back, fingers the crumpled, heavy-gauge plastic Throc laid down in case the baby comes while Russell's at work and Norma delivers in transit. It occurs to Russell that the highlighted map in her hospital bag may be for Throc. Maybe she expects Russell to be gone.

One of Throc's daughters, three or four years old, scurries into Russell's lap. He can't remember her name. "Good morning," he says.

"Russell," she says.

A smaller girl up front stands in the seat and looks back at Russell like she might cry. She reaches out and yanks the hair of the girl on Russell's lap. It's clear that he's spoiled some arrangement by not sitting in front. Throc smiles at each girl, laughs in a way that says it's okay, whatever it is. "I want to sit your lap," the girl standing in front says. Then Norma gets in up front and the girl seems satisfied with that. She puts her cheek against Norma's belly and is still.

Throc starts the car and the engine whispers somewhere beneath them like doves in a cote. "Hi," he smiles. "Hi."

The car phone rings. Norma answers, waits a beat, says, "He's here, sugar. Everything's fine." Norma calls her mother sugar. Ordinarily this steams Russell, coming as it will after he answers the phone and endures Hannah's starchy silence, but now it's somehow a comfort. "It wasn't his fault," Norma says. "He was a victim." She nods, listens. "I have to go, sugar. You'll know when it's time." She listens again, waits. "You'll just *know*."

It occurs to Russell that he should take Norma straight to Hannah's, or to the hospital maybe, tell her it's okay to have the baby now, then stash himself on a Greyhound bus to anywhere, someplace far. Who could argue she wouldn't be better off?

They're not inside the apartment two seconds when Throc's happy voice upstairs pierces the morning like the Fourth of July. "Hi! Oh, hi, hi, hi!" Tiny voices shriek, footsteps rain down the stairs, small fists flail at the door. "Russell! Russell!"

A terrible noise falls from above, heavy clomps and groaning. Hairball coils up on the kitchen counter, his wild eyes locked on the sag overhead. "What is it?" Norma asks. "What's happening?"

Russell opens the door and Throc's girls take his hands, pull him outside. "Russell! Come, come!"

"Don't leave!" Norma says. "Call the police!"

"No," Russell says. "It's okay. Stay here."

He follows the girls upstairs to Throc's apartment, finds Throc nose to nose with a cow in the living room, laughing. The cow's eyes flash to Russell, wide and nervous, seeing all but understanding nothing. That's how cow eyes are though, aren't they?

"Somebody put me a cow!" Throc says. "Hi!"

"It's okay," Russell says, his heart slowing, finding its normal rhythm. "It's just a prank. Those guys have got your number, Throc."

"This good one," Throc says. "Look! Look her there!" He points to the cow's side. Throc's girls part for Russell and he sees first the pink glare, then the working, pulsing motion of organs behind glass. It's a cow with a window.

Russell kneels down, Throc's carpet is still damp from the flood and spongy beneath his bad knees. With the soft pad of his finger he traces the cow's tight, well-healed stitches, strokes the glass, which is some sort of Plexi, actually feels the warm coursing of fluids. The animal shifts nervously, but Throc's girls smooth the hair at her flanks, rub her side. Throc picks up his littlest daughter — Bao is her name — and she gently caresses the slope of the cow's nose, between her eyes, and across the swell of her frightened brow.

Russell heard of cow windows when he worked for three days once at a dairy. He didn't see one but he imagined it, and now it's here, in Throc's upstairs apartment. Which reminds him of something stranger yet: that cows can walk up stairs but not down. Throc's laughing — he knows — so what the hell, Russell laughs too. What's a man supposed to do?

"Russell?"

Norma's standing in Throc's doorway. Russell waves her over, says, "It's a cow. A cow with a view." Norma comes closer, and Russell shows her.

"This is going to sound weird," Norma says, "but I knew there was going to be a cow up here."

"Good sign," Throc says, nodding. "It's good."

"Did you know it would have a window in it?" Russell asks Norma. He's not cracking wise, he really wants to know.

She thinks for a second. "No," she says. "That part's a surprise."

Russell takes one of the cow's teats, tries to recall his milking grip. He squeezes two, three times before a stream piddles onto Throc's carpet.

"Taste it," Norma says.

Russell catches a drop, licks his finger. "It's milk," he says. He takes Norma's hand in his, holds it to the Plexiglas in the cow's side and closes his eyes. "Feel," he says. Norma closes her eyes too. Together they imagine the baby, Norma's nipples, swollen and brown like hazelnuts, a dribble of milk, little lips and gums and foggy blue eyes, a sprinkle of pale hair and the soft pulse beneath it.

"When you didn't come home last night I thought you left," Norma says.

"I know," Russell says. "I was just in jail, though."

Norma squeezes his hand. "I'm glad."

Back in their apartment, Russell spreads the cushions out on the floor and Norma lies down, clicks the TV on and drifts off to sleep. Russell lies beside her, makes a *kiss kiss* noise to Hairball on the kitchen counter, who merely glances at him, annoyed.

In his head, Russell drives the route to the hospital — the one highlighted on Norma's map — only it's Throc's New Yorker he's driving, not his van, so it's quiet except for the lowing of the air conditioner, smooth. Then a thunderous *moo* pounds the ceiling. Hairball springs into the air and swipes at the bulb of rot, then falls to the floor in a shower of pulp and dust and ruddy goop. Norma's eyes snap open and she grabs Russell's hand. She says, "Something's happening, Russell. I can feel it."

my best day was
the third grade

YORG MALIK was having a time with his stutter. It took him nearly all morning to say "The British are coming," but when he was done it took me only seconds of top quality mimicry to have him in tears. Mrs. Keedy scolded me viciously, and I cried. Then I saw Heidi Van Arsdale rubbing herself in that place with a crayon. When I announced it to the class, though, she said I was lying, and I had to pull her dress up to let everyone see the periwinkle scribblings for themselves. Mrs. Keedy made Heidi go to the bathroom and wash out her underwear, but Heidi threw them in the trash instead and went without. I know because I bent down to check her work when she returned. I made no new announcement about this, but my secret knowledge kept me occupied until noon.

For lunch, we were lined up as usual for our march to the cafeteria, but as I was at the end of the line it was easy for Henry Rodriguez and Troy Kupp to lag behind and beat me up before I reached the door. Heidi Van Arsdale stayed to watch, which was upsetting because I thought we'd shared something. The beating didn't take long. It didn't hurt much either, but I cried anyway. This seemed to make Henry and Troy happy, and that in turn made me happy because I wanted to be liked.

After school, Jimmy Yehudi asked me to his house to play. He said nobody would play with him because he was Jewish, which I thought meant he threw up a lot. Jimmy had every imaginable form of recreation in his basement. The Ping-Pong table was my favorite. The paddles were thick and cushiony. After we played all the games, Jimmy invited me to sleep over. I didn't, but before I left I made a deal to trade him my secondhand Big Jim camping set, which I cried about receiving as a birthday gift, for his magnetic hockey game. Jimmy said his mom wouldn't let him trade stuff. I told him to get on a kitchen chair and lick the frost off the freezer, it tastes like cherry. He did. Then I told him I'd get him unstuck if he traded. He agreed, so I kicked the chair out from under him. I took the hockey game and left, but not before I slipped a Ping-Pong paddle under my shirt.

That night my dad, who was my mom's fourth and best husband, took me to the Pinewood Derby for Chicago-area Cub Scouts. My uniform was bare because I'd earned no badges in the seven months we'd lived there, not even the safety badge, which was practically a freebie. The race was a big deal. It was at the fairgrounds. Jimmy Yehudi was there with his dad too. His car was slick with silver paint and detailed appliqués. He came in second for the whole city. His dad had put liquid mercury in the nose of his car. My car was knocked out in the first race. It took fourth out of four cars. It sported its original pine finish and a lead fishing weight taped into its hollow rear. It rattled like a Sucrets tin coming down the long wooden ramp. Jimmy's trophy was bigger than my leg.

Ginger, the most stunning girl in my school, was playing on the snowman in front of our apartment building when I got home. She and I and my mom had built it months ago with the first snow I'd ever seen. It was solid ice now. Ginger followed my dad and me down to our basement apartment. I told her I lost the race. She kissed me on the lips, real quietly. She didn't know what to do then, so she punched me lightly on the nose. I didn't know what to do either, so I cried. She ran away, and my heart soared remembering the kiss. I went inside and gave the Big Jim doll a vagina with a steak knife. The next day at school I gave the doll to Jimmy Yehudi as promised. I told everyone he'd thrown up buckets the day before. He threw Big Jim and hit me in the ear. He was crying, and I cried too. I was feeling good.

The next summer we moved back to Lodi. When the bus pulled into the Oakland station my dad and I got off. He said he'd enjoyed being my dad. He was crying. I got back on the bus and my mom gave me a look, like she always did when things changed. I told myself I'd never cry again, and I haven't.

Why am I remembering this? Because I saw Jimmy Yehudi last night. I am rich now and live in Chicago once again. I have season tickets to Bulls games and hardly ever go. But last night I went. Chicago is not the same, so I went to the Stadium, where things are fast and bright. The Bulls were losing and I yelled for popcorn. Jimmy bounded up the steps and sold it to me. His nametag said only *Jim*, but it was him. He didn't recognize me, didn't lift his eyes once, not even when he asked if I wanted change back.

I was crying when I got home, as I have been now for almost twenty-four hours. My wife, who is beautiful, more than Ginger and Heidi Van Arsdale put together, cannot console me. I think I might feel better if I throw up, but I can't, or at any rate won't. Whatever is inside me, call it popcorn, is stuck there. Maybe it will never come out. If it doesn't, that's okay. I have paid for it and it is mine, no more or less than what I owe, or what is owed me.

blood work

ONE AFTERNOON while making my pickups for the lab, I found myself alone on the road, my spirit empty as the summer San Joaquin sky. I was thinking of quitting my job but wasn't sure. The lab wasn't the same with Roy gone and his widow, Gwen, in charge. I was unskilled labor — about that I had no illusions — but now I felt judged, ranked. So as man has done for as long as he's walked the earth — thousands of years or millions, depending on your source — I looked to the sky for answers.

Then I heard screams and a hunched-over old woman reared up suddenly before me. I braked hard, the back end of my ancient Toyota kicking out sideways and skidding to a stop. The little Coleman cooler jumped from the seat beside me and smacked the glove box. Then I saw the stop sign, the crosswalk, the school children at the woman's heels. The machinery of my heart seized up and I sat shaken as her eyes locked to mine. She waved the children by, and when they were a good distance down the street, she shrank back into her crouch, lowered her hand-held sign, and turned me loose. "You shouldn't be driving," she called out as I passed.

Immediately I pulled to the curb and peeked inside the Coleman: Three separator tubes lay broken from the crash, the bricks of blue ice slick with human serum. The carriage of blood was no longer my business.

I drove immediately home and dumped the contents of the Coleman into a Zip-loc bag and put it in the refrigerator. Mom was watching Court TV from her chair. "What are you doing?" she hollered.

"You don't want to know," I said.

"Well do it quieter."

I washed the Coleman in the sink, softly, then went to my room. I had more thinking to do.

A while later Mom banged on my door. "Who are you talking to?" she asked.

I didn't know I was talking, but that wasn't uncommon.

"No one," I said.

"Are you praying again?"

"No," I said. "Sort of. Leave me alone."

"Do me a favor," she said. "Lie to me next time."

Technically, I do not pray. I don't go to church, read the Bible, the Koran, the Talmud or Torah, the I Ching, Ram Dass, horoscopes, the Book of the Dead or Ayn Rand. (When I read, it's usually *US News* or mild pornography.) I of course talk to God, but in conversation. I say, "Hey, God, how am I doing?" or "How's tricks?" When Roy died by his own hand, I said, "God, my friend was seduced by the quick fix. Don't let it cost him his place in Heaven. Instead, let it bring him peace."

God held up His end of the conversation pretty well, and I'd become a fair hand at hearing His voice in the clutter, feeling His hand on mine. We had rapport. He didn't speak in words of course — I'm no loon — but through the ironic sign, irony being the last strain of divine voice we'll hear before psychiatric help.

An example: Some minutes after I recommended Roy to the here-after — I'd been counting chlamydia kits in the storage room — I was called to the phone. When I picked up, there was no one there, only that smooth, steady drone, as sonorous a sound as you'll find inside city limits. Now come on. It doesn't take a saint to see.

Before my mother's interruption, I'd been angling for precise indication — a heavenly mandate toward, say, air conditioning repair. But also I was kicking around the big questions — why, who, when? Lately I'd been wishing that I had a child to feed, a grandmother needing surgery, something to say, *This is what I'm doing it for.* But I had only me. Mom figured I was still finding myself, and as long as I did it quietly she didn't begrudge me a long search. But to me the opposite seemed true: The more I looked around, the more lost I became. I thought perhaps I'd found my place at the lab — a helping profession — but that morning at work, before my near collision with fate, I'd realized I was wrong.

From the moment the doors opened at eight, patient traffic was slow — a few blood counts, an allergy screen, a serum pregnancy. My early route to the doctors' offices yielded only two vaginal swabs and a Hemoccult, a foil packet of stool to be checked for blood. Gwen paced the floor, worrying the hem of her blazer. When the bookkeeper came in, Gwen corralled him into the office. Her crying was soon audible through the door. We all listened, embarrassed but also smugly satisfied. Gwen's first act after taking over the lab was to cut everyone's pay, then she threw a lavish open house party for doctors to court their business. Employees, by memo, were uninvited.

When she came out of the office, her eyes puffy, everyone guiltily shifted into make-work mode, trying to give the appearance of value for our wage. The techs ran bogus protocols. The phlebotomists, Penny and Matthew, practiced on each other until their arms were striped with Band-Aids, a shameful sight. I vacuumed the carpets and emptied the wastebaskets, not in my job description but tasks to which I wasn't averse. Certainly I was no better a man than the janitor, though I'd never made his acquaintance.

The fat-testing machine arrived after lunch, and Gwen greeted it like the Holy Ghost. "Thank God. I thought it wouldn't come." The machine was part of the wellness program she was launching that night, a body-fat test and cholesterol screen marketed through health clubs and businesses. Everyone, even the techs, crowded into the drawing room to check the machine out. It was a disappointment, a glorified ohmmeter with two electrodes, one that attached to a finger and one to a toe. I breezed through the user's manual; pretty scant for such a fussy industry. The machine sent a tiny electrical charge through the body and measured the resistance, which determined the fat percentage. Something grander had been expected. Matthew shook the box and a floppy disk fell out. Gwen deflated.

"Why not let's give her a try," Matthew said.

"Why is it a 'her'?" Penny asked.

Matthew sighed. "Pumpkinseed, join the war for the personal pronoun, won't you? We're just a hop, skip, and a Republican away from clitoridectomies and jackbooted clergy in every bedroom. How about let's hop on board, okay?"

Penny rolled her eyes. "Why would anyone want their fat quantified? Isn't the idea to keep it a secret?"

"It's like the first level of the AA cabal," Matthew said. "It forces you to look in the mirror and be honest. 'Hips like a milk jug — check.' Then you submit to whatever torture will fix it."

"What if you're supposed to have milk-jug hips?"

Matthew slumped in his smock. "Then I guess you could go to the movies."

"What if you've seen everything?" I asked.

Phlebotomists were beneath techs on the med-lab chain of being, but couriers were smack at the bottom. "Then maybe you should get back to work," Matthew said. "Unless you want your fat — what did you say, Penny — oh yes, *quantified.*"

"It's okay with me," I said. "I'll do it." I kicked off a shoe and peeled away my sock.

Benny, the head tech, cracked wise. "Don't you have stool samples to fetch?"

"Why?" I asked. "You hungry?"

"Grow up," Gwen barked. "Both of you." She slipped off her blazer and lay back on the gurney. "Someone hook me up."

Penny and Matthew stared blankly at each other. Matthew set the machine on the gurney beside Gwen and fumbled with the electrodes. Finally Penny took them from him and pushed him away. Penny had been with the lab forever. She was a good phlebotomist, painless. She clipped an electrode to Gwen's finger, then tugged at her nyloned foot. "These have to come off."

Gwen paid the techs, Penny, and the boisterously gay Matthew no mind, but at me she stared as if I should turn around or, preferably, leave. "Do you mind?"

"Why just me?" I asked.

"Because you're a fecal boy," Benny said.

"Just leave," Matthew said. "Drive something somewhere."

"He's a medical professional," Penny said.

Gwen narrowed her eyes, unwavering.

As strong an impulse as I've ever felt grabbed me then and

rooted me to that spot, my eyes to her pale, upturned feet. *Erection!* some might cry. But that wasn't it. It was *insurrection*, my boat-rocking nature holding fast against snobbery and injustice. Gwen's tears had earlier moved me to labor, but driven by the whip, I was unbending.

She waited a beat. "Fine." She reached beneath her skirt, hiking it without regard, and pulled off her nylons. I didn't look especially, but neither did I look away.

Penny roughly clipped the wire to her pinkie toe and pushed the button on the machine. She waited. "It's not working."

"Did you push the right button?" Gwen asked.

"There's only one."

I stepped forward then. "Don't worry," I said. "I worked at Radio Shack." I rapped the machine with a knuckle and the number instantly appeared. "Twenty-eight percent," I said. "That's pretty good for a girl."

Gwen tensed. "How about for an employer?"

"Yeah," I said, "for them too."

I turned to leave and she shifted on the gurney to reinstall her hose, the *woosh* of good fabric against smooth skin behind me. "Thanks for your *professional* help," she said.

My mother knocked again at the door. "Someone's here for you," she said. "A woman. What could she want?"

It was Gwen. "What happened to you?" she asked. "Didn't you make your route?"

"Partways," I said. "I think I have to quit the lab, though."

"Quit? Why?"

"I just think I'm supposed to. It's my time." This seemed a clumsy choice of words in light of Roy. "Come in," I said. "Have something to drink."

Gwen dragged into the house behind me. "Just give me the samples," she said. "One of the techs is waiting, an hour into overtime, thank you very much."

"I'm sorry," I said. "I almost hit some kids with my car. It was a sign that I need to change direction."

"A sign. You're religious, aren't you?"

"That question just leads to trouble. I follow directions when I get them, how's that?"

"Penny quit today too. Is that a sign, do you think?"

"I don't know. Does it mean anything to you?"

"Yeah, it means I don't have anyone to draw blood for the wellness test tonight. And with no notice, either. Just boom, gone. Don't you people plan anything?"

You people. I ignored this. "I'm sorry."

"Boom," Gwen said. "Now you're gone, too."

"I'm sorry about Roy," I said. "I don't think I ever told you that."

"My daughter refuses to sleep at night because she thinks I'm going to leave her too. How can I convince her I'm not? She's six years old."

"Just keep being there when she wakes up, I guess."

"Sometimes it feels like I *am* going away. Or everything else is going away from me." Her look hardened then. "Just give me the samples. I have to go."

"Stay for dinner," I said. "Please."

"I can't. I have the wellness testing tonight. And I don't date my employees."

"I'm not your employee anymore," I reminded her. "And it's not a date. It's food."

"Just give me the samples. I'm tired."

"Come on, stay. Mom," I called out. "What's for dinner?"

Mom rearranged herself in her chair and harumphed. "Whatever's in the fridge."

"Hm. Let's eat out."

"I'm not eating with my daughter tonight," Gwen said. "And all those rich people haven't eaten all day for the fat test. I can't not show up."

"If I can ask, what makes you think the wellness thing will work? They do cholesterol testing at Long's and Payless and everywhere else for, like, five bucks."

"Yeah," she said. "But those tests are worthless. You're supposed to fast for twenty-four hours. You eat a Jumbo Jack before those cheapy tests and you have Jumbo Jack blood — lots of fat, lots of cholesterol, but it means nothing."

"Still," I said. "It's a hard thing to get excited about."

"That's why the fat-testing machine," Gwen continued, animated now. "That's the hook. It's 99.8% accurate, almost as good as a dunk tank. You picture beautiful bodies all over your advertising, sell the sizzle, not the steak. It's an impulse buy. You show the personalized diet printout they get; it's impressive. Actually, that part's sort of standardized. There are only four different results, and they're based on how much salt you're willing to give up, not on body fat per se."

"What good is the impulse buy of the fat test if you have to fast for the cholesterol part?" I asked.

Gwen nodded. "That's where the plan wobbles," she said. "The cholesterol test is more worthwhile, but it doesn't sizzle."

"Oh."

"Yeah. That's about what everyone has said so far. 'Oh.' And now Penny quit so I don't have anyone to draw blood tonight. Matthew's got his midwife training class. Will you help me?"

"I'm not a phlebotomist."

"I'll handle that part," Gwen said. "I've played around with it, it's easy. That's why it doesn't pay much." Then Gwen took my hand, or more accurately, put hers in mine. It was warm and smooth. "Please," she said. "I need you."

The health club was across town from the lab, and Gwen forgot to bring the folding table for the fat-test customers to lie on. The club manager provided an armchair, which was fine for the blood-drawing — sit down, bend your arm, no big deal — but the body-fat test required the supine position. Gwen would have to ask the customers to lie on the floor. It was an embarrassment made worse by the fact that we'd be conducting the tests in full, windowed view of the club's membership. "To give it a sense of event," the club manager said, pointing with an expensive pen to a racquetball court with a Plexiglas wall. It was the focal point of the club's lounge, a monolith of white light faced by dozens of overstuffed armchairs and leather couches — a stage, nothing less. A public embrace of vanity.

For a while it didn't look like I'd have much fat to quantify, and not because of a particularly lean clientele; the gig simply seemed a bust. After a brief initial rush — a half-dozen or so impatient fasters who made a beeline for the snack bar the instant their blood was drawn and their fat sounded — the patronage slowed to zero. Gwen sat against the wall looking forlorn, watching the comings and goings of the membership through the Plexiglas. People looked in at the haphazard sprawl of blood-drawing and fat-measuring apparatus but avoided eye contact.

After an hour or so of silence made crushing by the huge room, a very stylish head peeked in through the section of back wall that was actually the door. The man's hair was light blond tapering at a sharp angle to Taster's Choice brown, crystals and all. "Gotta fast for this thing, huh?"

I nodded, and was about to use Gwen's line about Jumbo Jack blood — pretty good pitch, that — but she interrupted. "It's more accurate if you do," she said, "but not essential."

A shame, thought I. Business made it hard for a person to keep her integrity. Which was why I didn't bemoan my bottom rung on the labor ladder: It was easy to keep your soul off the market when the price offered was only pennies.

The hairdo man looked skeptical. He was fortyish, clearly fit. He came in and stripped off his shirt though no one had asked him to. "Okay," he said, "let's do it."

Gwen drew his blood, his jaw muscles clenching when she touched the needle home. Then he lay on the floor for the fat test. I removed his shoe and sock, wiped his big toe with an antiseptic towelette from a foil pouch. He said, "Dunk-tank accuracy, huh? Wouldn't happen to have proof of that, would you?"

"Not on me," I said.

"Thought so."

"If you want, I'll have a copy of the test diagrammatics left at the front desk for you."

"That's all right," he said. "I'll live."

Diagrammatics. Sometimes I slay myself.

Another customer came in then, a woman in one of those garish, silky warm-up suits in colors only the moneyed concern them- selves with — taupe, salmon, celadon maybe. Gwen introduced herself and explained the procedure.

"Your name sounds very familiar," the woman said to Gwen. Gwen asked the woman her name. "Sheila Crown," she replied.

Gwen's cardboard smile folded. "You work for Clovis Unified Schools," she said.

"Yes," Sheila Crown said.

"Human resources."

Hairdo turned toward the two women, interested now. Sheila Crown looked suspicious. "Yes."

"I called your office a few times about wellness testing for your employees. I came by once or twice, left some literature."

Sheila Crown's eyes dropped to the floor. "Yes," she said. An awkward beat or two passed, then Sheila Crown pressed a smile into service. "So, this is the program you were selling?"

Gwen nodded weakly. She looked over at me — I was removing the electrodes from Hairdo's toe. I pumped my fist, urging her on. She took a deep breath; the set of her shoulders hardened. Both her manner and gaze were at once direct. "Yes," she said to Sheila Crown. "That's right. I think it's something you should seriously consider."

"Why is that?" Sheila Crown asked.

"You underwrite your own health insurance, right?"

"Yes."

"That means every time one of your employees goes to the doctor or gets sick or, God forbid, has a heart attack or high blood pressure or any of the conditions we now know are linked to cholesterol and body weight, the expense of diagnosing and treating that condition comes directly out of your pocket. This is a preventive program designed to keep your employees at work and out of the doctor's office."

"Hm." Sheila Crown fussed with the drawstring of her suit. "Public schools can't afford —"

"I realize that," Gwen interrupted. "Believe me, I do. Especially in California. But that's the best part of this program. It doesn't cost the schools a dime. It's a voluntary program, very inexpensive, paid for by whichever employees choose to participate. All I need is the opportunity to present the program to them. My laboratory will send a team to each of the schools to perform the tests, which the employees can take before school. Or after."

"Taking her shot, isn't she?" Hairdo chuckled.

Sheila Crown removed her flouncy jacket. "Well. Maybe. If we could get started here?"

"Please," Gwen said, helping Sheila with her sleeves. She ushered her with a firm hand into the drawing chair, smiling fiercely.

"I should tell you," Sheila Crown said, "I have submerged veins. They always have a hard time finding one. They're in there somewhere, I'm told, but if you can't find one just say so."

Catastrophe had the eye of a bully in seeking out the weak. Nearly everyone had grimaced in pain at Gwen's needlework, far beyond the ordinary — customers rubbing their arms up to the shoulder, even favoring one side as they walked away. One older man, who came in bragging about the ubiquity and strength of his veins, relating praise his doctors had heaped on him for his needle-friendly circulatory system, leaked a hard-fought tear when Gwen stuck him. Surprisingly, I thought, she didn't seem at all cowed by Sheila Crown's deep veins. The bright lights of her smile shone full bore.

After tying Sheila Crown's arm off, Gwen prodded the pit of her elbow. She slapped her forearm a few times with her fingers, trying to rub a vein up. From what I'd seen at the lab, that usually did it. Gwen seemed satisfied. She steadied the needle above Sheila's arm and pushed it in.

Sheila Crown jerked quickly away, sucking air through her

teeth. "I don't think that was it," she said. She laid her arm back down, bravely offering it once more. Gwen aimed, then stuck her again. Sheila Crown grimaced, her arm steady but the rest of her body writhing. "Oh. Oh." Gwen seemed to be digging deep, searching. My own arm twinged at the sight, and I may have even repeated after her. *Oh!*

Hairdo's face contorted as he watched. "That hurts," he said.

I jotted down his fat percentage — seventeen. "You're through." He looked disappointed. He slipped on his socks and shoes, and seconds after he left the court I saw him outside the glass wall, looking on from one of the club's cushiony chairs. He waved to two women sitting at the bar, and they joined him at the Plexiglas.

Gwen's face was a study of concentration now. "Please," Sheila said. "That's fine." She withdrew her arm. "I guess they're just not out tonight."

"I *know* I can get it," Gwen said. She looked angry, gripping the rig of needle and tube as though to plunge it into her own thigh. She needed help.

Audibly, but not with force, my stomach growled. "Pardon me," I said. "I skipped dinner."

"I haven't eaten for twenty-four hours," Sheila Crown said. "I could eat six hot dogs laid end to end without taking a breath."

"A hot dog does sound good," I agreed. I pointed to the fat-test machine. "Do you want to at least have this done?"

Sheila Crown shook her head. "I don't really care about that part," she said. "I know how much fat I have, believe me. I just wanted my cholesterol done right." She sighed. "But now I just want to eat."

Then my stomach growled again, this time a booming, guttural moan that ripped through the chambered silence like an avalanche, an epochal upheaval of glacial ice. It was a sign, and at once I understood what it meant. I took the needle from Gwen and approached Sheila Crown. "Would you mind if I tried?"

Gwen looked at me and shook her head, subtly but firmly. *No!*

"Okay," Sheila Crown said. "It's a shame to waste a good fast."

I took hold of her arm, lightly tracing my fingertips over its faint blue lines. I hesitated at the joint of her forearm and biceps, at the marks from Gwen's last attempt. "Are you sore here?" I asked her.

"Nah," Sheila said. "I'm tough."

None of her veins looked sturdy enough. I let loose of that arm and took up her other one, made a tight cusp with one hand around her biceps. It didn't look good. I glanced over at Gwen again, and again she shook her head, more pointedly than before. *Absolutely not!*

"Would you mind trying this another way?" I asked.

Sheila Crown lay on a sheet on the wood floor of the racquetball court, naked from the waist down except for powder blue cotton briefs. I knelt at her feet. Gwen held up a sheet between Sheila and me and the small audience now milling in groups outside the Plexiglas wall, staring in. Sheila Crown fidgeted, watching me with nervous, unblinking eyes. Gwen looked on with a blank expression as if lost. She was out of it now, except for legally.

I spread apart each of Sheila's toes and explored the crevices with my finger. People shot heroin between their toes, I knew from TV, so there had to be veins there. I found not a one, though.

"I'm very uncomfortable about this," Sheila said.

"So am I," said Gwen.

"Don't even tell me if you're not licensed to do this," Sheila said.

"I won't," I said.

"He's not," Gwen said.

Sheila closed her eyes. "I can't believe I'm doing this."

"I won't try it if I don't think I can do it," I said.

She grabbed two fistfuls of sheet beneath her. "Go ahead," she said. "I don't want to fast again any time soon. I don't know how the Arabs do it."

"Ramadan," I said. I lifted Sheila's leg and rested her foot on my shoulder. "They believe."

Deep in the flesh of Sheila Crown's inner thigh, I found a hint of pale blue angling down her leg. With my finger, I traced it the length of her thigh, lost it in the pit behind her knee, but picked it up again on her lower calf, a darker, closer blue now than before. She gripped and regripped the sheet, anxious. I felt as if I could become so myself.

"Did you know Arabs have higher cholesterol than other people?" I asked her.

She looked puzzled. "Why?"

"I don't know, they just do. Counts of three hundred or even higher. And it doesn't mean anything. They can be perfectly healthy in every way, just with high cholesterol."

"They don't have to cut down on salt?"

"Nope."

"Why do you know that?" Gwen asked.

I shrugged. You hang around a med lab, you pick things up. I didn't say this in front of Sheila Crown, though.

I closed my eyes again and let my fingers wander the length of

Sheila Crown's leg, waiting, praying, even, for the same guiding hand that made me take the damn needle in the first place. It was time to receive it again, and I trusted that it would come. I would feel heat, an impulse toward specific movement, direction. Like water-witching.

Gwen started giggling. She said, "Use the force, Luke." Something had crossed over in her. She now wore the reckless grin of someone with nothing to lose, though she still had plenty.

Sheila said, "If you can't find one —"

"I think I've got one," I said. I pressed my finger to a spot in her ankle. The vein actually disappeared an inch or two higher, but its path suggested that it would find its way here, to this spot. I wasn't at all sure, but it seemed that higher up on the leg would be too painful a place to stick a needle. It was here and now or not at all.

"I'm kind of nervous," Sheila Crown said. "Tell me something else, like about the Arabs."

"There're a lot of people watching," Gwen said. "I think they're wondering what we're doing to you."

"That doesn't exactly relax me," Sheila said. "Tell me a joke."

"I never remember jokes," Gwen said.

"Then tell us a story," I said.

"A story?"

Sheila watched in naked dread as I lined up the cotton swabs, alcohol, and tape. She looked up at Gwen. "Any story," she said.

"A story," Gwen said. "Well . . . oh, I've got one. This couple I know — this is funny when you think about it — they're on vacation. In Hawaii, let's say. One day they come back to their hotel room to find things shifted around, different than how they left them. Nothing's missing, though, so they chalk it up to housekeeping and go on with their fun. When they get home and have the pictures from their trip developed, there are pictures taken inside their hotel room of men's bare butts. They look close and see their toothbrushes sticking out of the men's butts. Can you imagine?"

"Oh my God," Sheila said. "What did they do?"

"Nothing," Gwen said. "What could they do?"

Matthew told this story in the lab the other day. It happened to friends of friends, he said, in Bermuda, though, not Hawaii. He told everyone. They all laughed and made bitter faces.

"These are people you know?" I asked.

"Well," Gwen said, "friends of friends."

"When I heard it in high school," I said, "it was a mob guy that happened to. He killed the hotel manager."

Gwen's smile fell. "Does that make you feel superior?" she asked.

"No," I said.

I dug my thumbnail slightly into Sheila's skin, close to the target point. That's what Penny did with people before she inserted the needle; the pressure redirected their attention, prepared them. I slid the needle in and Sheila sucked air in quick puffs. Blood dribbled into the vacuum tube.

"I know it wasn't my story," Gwen said, "but even as Matthew was telling it, it felt like it was. Roy and I — that's my husband," she said to Sheila, "*was* my husband — anyway, we went to Hawaii a few months ago, right before his accident. We were having some problems and we thought, you know, a vacation. So we stayed at the Laguna Maui, very ritzy-titsy. We couldn't afford the trip but it seemed important. And oh, it did the trick for a while. Snorkel, snorkel, snorkel; sail, sail, sail. And eat? Oh my God. We were turning things around, it seemed. Really." She sighed. "But when we got back to Fresno, everything was exactly the same as when we left. Nothing had changed; we were fooling ourselves. When the pictures from the trip came back a few days later, Roy sat on the floor, crying and looking through them. He said, 'I've never seen these people before in my life,' and tore them all into tiny pieces."

Sheila breathed in and out, in and out, eyes closed to the pain. I slipped the needle free of her ankle to the *pat pat* of Gwen's tears on the hardwood floor and taped a cotton ball over the wound. It was done.

"That's a nicer story," Sheila said. "Sad, but nice."

The fully clothed Sheila stood and gave a thumbs up to the crowd outside. A smattering of applause padded through the Plexiglas. Gwen faced her audience and took a bow. Sheila said she'd ask around the school district office about the wellness program, see if there was any interest. Gwen seemed happy with that. It was a fair shot. "And you," Sheila said to me, "you get a license if you're going to stick needles in people's legs." She tried but failed to hold back a playful smile.

"I'm just a driver," I said. "I don't even have a license for *that*."

The club members started coming in for testing then, and kept up in a steady stream all night. Many of them asked if it was okay that they hadn't fasted like the sign said they were supposed to. I assured each of them that it was fine, still a very accurate test. I declined Gwen's offer to take over the blood drawing and instead wired fingers and toes until the last customer was gone.

As we cleaned up, Gwen asked why I'd closed my eyes before sticking Sheila Crown. "You were waiting for a sign, weren't you?"

"I was," I said. "But it didn't come."

"What do you mean? You did great."

"I faked it and got lucky. That's not the way I do things. I could have hurt her."

"You weren't faking," she said. "I saw you."

"You should sell the lab," I said.

"Sell it?" Gwen narrowed her eyes in disbelief. "You really are a child, aren't you? Roy ran the lab for years at a loss. All I own is debt. I have no choice but to make it work."

In that moment, the world got bigger. My opposition to the unnatural order of its workings seemed suddenly small and apologetic. Childish, as Gwen suggested. Yet I still believed that I was right.

"I met payroll tonight," Gwen continued. "If this program takes off, I can put everyone's salaries back. Raise them, even. This could work."

I use the word "God" because this is America and I like to think that way, but whether you want to call it providence or the universe, instinct or reason, gut feeling or blind, deaf, and dumb luck, there is wisdom out there, and it will find you. But in its own time, not yours.

"Draw me," I said. The thought behind this wasn't mine, had never seen the gray of my brain nor the red blood that kept my heart from running dry. I simply opened my mouth like a ventriloquist's dummy and out came the words. "Draw me."

Gwen shrank from them. "I don't have to prove anything to you."

"I'm not here for a fat test," I said. "I'm a patient now. Draw me."

"I reserve the right to refuse service."

I laughed; it was funny. But then I sat in the chair and held out my arm. "Draw me."

"I'm not a phlebotomist," Gwen said. "You can't judge me by that."

"Blood is your business," I said. "Whether you chose it or not, I have to believe in you when you ask for it. I want to."

Gwen prepared the needle and vacuum tube. She testily swabbed my arm and rested her hand on it, about to stick me. I pulled away. "I'm sick," I said. "I don't know yet what it is, but something's wrong with me. Something's definitely not right. And I'm scared."

"You are?"

"I am."

Gwen took my arm again, softly this time. She flicked lightly at the vein, testing the elasticity of my skin. She brought the needle to me.

"It's going to hurt," I said. "I know that. But I can never really be prepared."

"That's not fair," she said. "I can't help it if it hurts. Sometimes things hurt."

"I know. But pretend it's your arm," I said. "Because it is."

Gwen was silent for a moment. She sneezed. Then she said, "Close your eyes." I closed them. She covered my hand with hers and lightly squeezed. "You're not alone," she said. She stroked my skin gently with her thumb. My anxieties, all my fears and uncertainties, trickled away. A firm but friendly pinch gouged my arm, then a sharp bite — the needle. Then Gwen's voice. "I'm with you," she said. Her voice echoed high and shining through the vast, empty room, unmistakable in the darkness. "You're not alone."

A cottony kiss at my arm, the tug of cloth tape. Then release. "I'm not alone," I said. I opened my eyes and it was true, I wasn't.

jarheads

A SUMMER FOG rolled through the drive-in like a huge gray tumbleweed and for a few minutes I couldn't see the screen or the big yellow Buick parked next to us or even Tommy, who was stretched out like a sheik on the hood of Quincy's car, drinking a can of Coors. I was standing next to Tommy, shaking my foot to hear the pebble in my shoe. It was the year I was trying to harden myself, become tough, and the pebble was a sharp reminder to walk with my toes turned inward. I'd read somewhere that pigeon-toed hitters have better balance in the batting box.

Being tough meant staying silent through the fog. I wanted to reach out to make sure Tommy was still beside me, but instead I listened to the pebble and waited. It was only fog. Just the same, I felt better when I heard Tommy's beer can crunch and hit the gravel in front of me. Quincy wasn't letting me drink because I was twelve, and though Tommy was just two years older, he lived in a house with both parents and always had pocket money and had to be home at six each night for dinner. When he talked to you he looked past you like you weren't really there. His dad was a pilot in the navy, an officer. In a small, poor town like ours — a service town for the nearby base — that stuff held sway with folks. Tommy wouldn't have taken pigeon-toes if he could have had them for nothing.

Quincy, who had been lying back against the windshield next to Tommy, said, "This is some fog." Then he laughed at something — I don't know what — but the sound seemed to come from the fog itself. "A weird night," Quincy said. "I like it."

Quincy was in the navy too. He lived on base. Tommy and I had just met him that afternoon. He was maybe the tallest person I'd ever seen. Without a doubt, the skinniest.

"It *is* weird," I said. "I like it too."

Then, as quick as it came in, the fog skipped on through, and there was Tommy again and Quincy and the yellow Buick beside us, full up with boys from the high school. Tommy was grinning at the screen. Cheech and Chong were driving a van made of marijuana. Sometime during the fog it had caught fire. Smoke billowed through the windows.

Quincy looked past Tommy and gave me a nod.

"Maybe you two should butt fuck," Tommy said.

The Buick rocked with laughter.

"What's your problem?" Quincy asked Tommy.

"No problem," Tommy said. "I'll take another one of those beers, though."

Quincy stared blankly at Tommy, then at me. He watched the movie for another minute or so then got down off the car and got Tommy a beer from the trunk. When he came back he said, "You guys ever smoke any of that wacky tobacco?"

Tommy lied. "Sure," he said.

I said I hadn't, lying in spirit if not in fact. The truth was, I grew up in rooms and cars full of grownups smoking pot. I'd seen my mother smoke it from glass tubes, brass pipes, even from another woman's mouth. More than once I'd felt a little hungry, just like they say.

"Well, you shouldn't," Quincy said. "Beer's one thing."

"My dad used to let us have a little beer," I said. "After we played baseball in my back yard."

"That was cool," Tommy said. "We always stuck him with Henson. We kicked their asses. Henson can't catch shit."

"Or hit," I said.

"Yeah," Tommy said. Then he smiled, kindly and sincerely. "Neither could your dad," he said.

"Yeah," I said.

Though I called him my dad, he was actually my stepdad, and anyway, he was dead. He hanged himself in the house we'd rented on Tommy's street, where we'd lived for seven months. After my dad was gone, my mom and I moved to an apartment we could afford alone. It was outside of town near the wrecking yard. Mom's new boyfriend, Stan, stayed with us most nights. Stan was a Marine.

"I don't know what the big deal about beer is," Quincy said. "It don't taste good." He held his can away from the car and emptied more than a little of it onto the ground. Then he threw it.

Tommy and I both laughed. Quincy threw like a little girl, all wrist and elbow.

"You got both ovaries behind that one," Tommy said.

Quincy got down off the car and grabbed Tommy by the shirt. "Listen —" he started, but Tommy held him up with just a look.

"Hands off, big guy," Tommy said. Then he leaned close to Quincy, like they were fast friends again. "Hey," he said. "There's pussy in the next movie."

Quincy looked doubtful, but he let Tommy go. "What do you know about pussy?" he said.

"What it tastes like," Tommy said.

Quincy laughed. "Like magazine paper?"

"Shit," Tommy said. "I get all I want. I should strap a mattress on my back to save time."

"Or on your front," I said.

Quincy turned to me, surprised. "Y'all talk like little itty-bitty children," he said. "You ain't seen shit and don't know shit, but you talk and talk and talk. Ain't *got* a damn thing to say."

"What about you?" Tommy asked Quincy. "You getting any?"

"Man," Quincy said, "I live in a barracks with over three hundred guys. What am I gonna get?"

Tommy and I had been in the arcade earlier that afternoon when Quincy asked us where the drive-in movie was. Tommy thought about directing him to bum fuck, I could tell from how he looked to me before answering, but then he told him the right way, and Quincy asked if we wanted to go with him. He said he'd buy beer, even pay for the movie. He asked how old were we and were we from here originally. It was his last night before shipping out for the Philippines, he said. A nine-month cruise. He said he was from Mississippi. "That was a slave state," I said. Tommy looked at me like I was stupid and embarrassing to have around, but Quincy slapped me on the shoulder. "I know," he said. "But it ain't no more." He gave us the rest of his quarters, almost five dollars in all, and said he'd be back for us later. When he was gone, Tommy said he was queer, you could tell from the way he walked, all floppy and bent over from grabbing his ankles. He said Quincy would probably try to cornhole us at the movies. I said we shouldn't go then, but Tommy said it would be okay, if he went for our rigs we could tell the theater manager and get him arrested. He said maybe we'd do that anyway. I said I didn't want to go, but Tommy pretended not to hear.

Quincy hadn't tried anything, though, and wasn't going to, but Tommy kept picking at him, trying to draw him out. Tommy could wear you down, make you see things his way.

"Are the barracks metal?" I asked Quincy.

"Metal?"

"Yeah. Like in *Gomer Pyle*?"

"Naw," Quincy said. "It's more like a big indoor apartment building. You get one room and one head, and you have to share it."

"You get head?" Tommy laughed. "Do you have to give it too?"

Quincy sighed.

"It's not metal?" I asked again.

"Nope," Quincy said. "Sorry. Concrete. Most military buildings are concrete."

"Metal ones would be neat in the rain," I said.

Quincy agreed that they would.

I was teaching myself mental discipline that summer too. When the first movie ended, a cartoon hot dog danced across the screen and laid itself down in a bun. Then a paper cup, a real one, filled itself as if by magic with Coca-Cola, shivering and fizzing through the tinny speaker hanging on the window. In my pocket I still had the two dollars my mom had left me for dinner. A hamburger with fries and a root beer cost $1.99 at the Snow Queen drive-in restaurant near our apartment. I took my dinners there. Werner, the old Swiss who owned the place, didn't charge me tax. Some days I arrived home from school to find that my mom had left me an extra dollar, which meant she'd made decent tips the night before. On those days I had either the Snow Queen Big Bargain (BBQ beef, large fries, large root beer) at $2.99 or funneled the extra money into the KISS pinball machine. I waited right up until I placed the order before deciding which. During school, I tried not to think too much about whether or not the extra dollar would be there. Once in a while I caught myself though, and if I realized that somewhere in my head the decision was made — pinball over more and better food, or vice versa — I condemned myself that night to the opposite choice.

The screen was blank while the second movie was being geared up. Though it was August, a chill had come down through the haze of tractor dust that hovered all summer over the flat San Joaquin Valley. I rubbed down the goose pimples on my legs. I was freezing, but glad I'd worn shorts instead of pants. I was teaching myself to adapt to circumstance.

"You hungry?" Quincy asked me.

"No."

"I am," he said. "This here is blackmail. They show us that ad then make us sit through a blank screen so we'll go buy an overpriced hot dog."

"Not everybody on base goes without pussy," Tommy said. He turned to me. "Ask him if he knows Stan."

"Who's Stan?" Quincy said.

"His mom's boyfriend," Tommy said. "He's a jarhead."

Though I'd tried to keep it a secret, Tommy knew about Stan. One morning he rode his bike across town to our new apartment without calling first like I'd asked. Stan answered the door wrapped in a bed sheet. He called me from my room and went back to chomping rings of pineapple and watching cartoons on the couch. A pall of pot smoke filled the room. My mom opened her bedroom door and peeked out. Tommy's stare shifted from Stan's water bong to my mom's black, swollen eye, then to the head-size hole in the wall beneath a store-bought cross-stitch that read *Home Is Where You Hang Your Hat.*

Stan moved the pipe behind the leg of the coffee table. He grinned up at us. "Helps my hangover," he said.

My mom tightened her robe at the throat and narrowed her eyes at me. "Who cares what the little prick thinks?" she said. Then she closed the door.

Quincy looked around Tommy to me. "So Stan ain't the base-ball-playing dad?" he asked.

I shook my head.

"His dad's deceased," Tommy said. He wanted to let fly with his theory about Stan and my mom killing my dad and making it look like suicide. I saw it in his eyes, the slow burn of the story heating up.

Quincy stared ahead at the empty screen. "It was my mom left me," he said. "She died when I was just little. Know what of?"

"No," I said.

"Want me to tell you?"

I nodded.

"A cold," Quincy said.

"You can't die from a cold," Tommy said.

"Sure you can," Quincy said. "If you don't do nothing about it. It turned into ammonia and she damn sure did die."

"*Pneu*monia," I said.

"What?"

"*Pneu*monia. I think it's pronounced with an *n*."

"That don't sound right," Quincy said. "But okay. Maybe I been saying it one way too long. Anyway, she had a real bad cough that wouldn't go away. It got louder and louder until one night my daddy told her, 'Shut up, you're just pining for attention.' She didn't cough no more after that. But then she died."

"How could she do that?" I asked. "Not cough?"

Quincy shrugged. "She knew Daddy."

Nobody said anything for a while. Quincy peeled dry skin from his lips. I kept an eye on Tommy, watched the torture of self-restraint in his eyes. He kept quiet though, and I was proud just then to have him for a friend. It was pure luck, of course — the fluke of my dad's job, living it up for even a little while in the house on Tommy's street — but being around Tommy had changed everything. I took on his confidence, his swagger. I told myself I'd never be the fawnlike little puss I was before.

"My dad hung himself," I said.

Quincy nodded. "Hm."

"He found out about Stan," Tommy said.

Then to me, Quincy said, "Why didn't he just whup him and her both?"

"I don't know," I said. "He didn't really fight or anything."

Quincy nodded. He clasped his hands behind his head and closed his eyes. A parade of expressions flashed across his face like he was telling himself a story. It struck me that he had a girl's face — small, sharp features like a doll. His nose was long and thin, flat at the tip, and his eyebrows were so slight they might have been penciled on. He looked like the glass angel my mom wrapped in tube socks and somehow managed to keep whole, Christmas after Christmas. As I stood watching Quincy, I tried to imagine him at sea with hundreds of men like Stan. But I couldn't do it. The picture just wouldn't come.

Quincy opened his eyes. "That don't mean there was something wrong with him. Meanness ain't like smarts. You can't study up on it or nothing."

Tommy pressed his beer into my chest when Quincy wasn't

looking. I didn't really want it, but it was a nod to our friend-ship, like me breaking the silence about my dad, so I took a big drink.

Quincy was right. It tasted bitter and stale. My eyes watered. I gave it back.

Quincy sat forward on the hood. "After my mom died," he said, "my daddy got *real* mean, and quicker than stink too. He was always sort of snappy, but her dying made him mad. After a while, my little brother ran away and I joined the service. Daddy got in his last knocks at me when he found out I went with the navy and not the Marines. That's what he done." Quincy looked at Tommy and started laughing. "He was a jarhead too."

"Jarhead," I repeated. The word felt funny in my mouth and I said it again. "Jarhead." Then Quincy caught on, and soon we were saying the word over and over. *Jarheads. Jarheads. Jarheads.* It was a funny sound when you could forget what it meant, and it got funnier every time we said it. I bet we said it a hundred times, laughing.

Finally Tommy jumped down from the car. He filled his cheeks with beer and spit it in a steady stream on Quincy's car. "My dad's a Marine," he said. I thought that was pretty dumb, because Tommy was the one who'd started it by calling Stan a jarhead, but Quincy must not have remembered. He just looked at Tommy and kept on laughing. "That don't surprise me one bit," he said.

When the second movie was over, the first one started up again. We weren't having fun anymore — Tommy had grown quiet — so after a while Quincy said, "I'm done with this. You boys ready to boogie?"

"I've got to leak first," Tommy said. He nodded for me to follow.

I waved him off, but he took me by the back of my neck and walked me away from the car.

"He's not going to try anything," I said.

"So?" Tommy said. He let loose of me but kept walking.

"So where are we going?"

"Just come on," he said.

"It's his last night here," I said.

Tommy stopped and faced me. He pressed his forehead hard against mine and pushed me backward. "Then go spend it with him," he said and walked off.

I called after him. "Where are you going?" He said nothing, just continued on toward the concession. I didn't know if he'd try to make trouble for Quincy or not, but I knew enough about him to be nervous.

I went back to the car and sat in the passenger seat. Quincy was still lying on the hood. He looked at me through the windshield. "Where's your buddy?" he said.

"He found some friends," I said. "He's going back to town with them." When Quincy didn't jump down right away, I said, "Let's leave. I have to go home."

Quincy got in the car and started the motor. He pumped the accelerator a few times and the engine roared. He adjusted his rear-view and looked around, for Tommy I imagined. "Friends, huh?" he said.

I nodded.

"What does that make you?" Quincy asked.

When we got to my apartment, the wristwatch hanging from Quincy's rear-view mirror said it was almost two. My mom wouldn't be home for a while yet. The Nite Kap would just now be closing and she'd have to clean up before she could leave.

"Which one's yours?" Quincy asked.

I pointed to our apartment. The light was on in the kitchen window. I'd turned it on before I left.

"Are you a pilot?" I asked Quincy, though I knew he wasn't.

"Not hardly," Quincy said. "I'm about as far under a pilot as I can be. When a pilot takes a crap, I salute the flies."

Quincy rolled down his window. "Listen to this," he said. He pushed a cassette tape into the player and mashed on buttons until he found the song he wanted. The music was slow at first, but it picked up — you could tell it was building toward something. Quincy sang along with it. He swayed from side to side like a cornstalk in the wind. I listened closely, trying to make myself feel what he felt. I couldn't do it.

When the song ended, Quincy's hands were trembling on the wheel. His breaths came in quick, shallow puffs, like he'd run a race. I pressed my cheek to the car window; it would have been wrong to look at him. The glass was cool, and when I blew my warm breath onto it, the word "fag" revealed itself in the brief steam. Tommy had put it there.

"Stan's going to be drunk," I said. "He's going to pick a fight with me for coming in this late."

Quincy didn't say anything for a minute, then he said, "Who's he to be picking fights?"

I shrugged.

Quincy snapped the radio off. "Where's his car?" he said. "Let's take a dump on the engine."

I scanned the parking lot for Stan's Super Sport. It wasn't there.

He was likely at the Nite Kap getting drunk and waiting for my mom to get off work. It was also likely that when they came back to the apartment, I wouldn't see them at all. They'd hole up in her room until the next afternoon when she would hurry off again to work. My mom was like that with men — binge, then purge, then binge again.

I pointed to a black Ford with a smashed bumper. "That's his," I said.

Quincy got out of the car. When I didn't, he got back in and said, "You okay?"

"Yeah," I said. And I was. But I was thinking about it being Quincy's last night before shipping out, how he'd spent it with two kids he didn't even know. My little self-improvement exercises seemed so childish. The pebble in my shoe.

I smeared the word "fag" off the window with my hand. "He beat her up last night," I said. But that didn't sound strong enough, so I said, "Us. He beat up both of us."

It was a lie, but when I saw Quincy deflate it felt true somehow. He said, "You want me to . . . you know, do something?" I told him I didn't, and he seemed relieved.

A burst of shouting erupted from somewhere, and some kids I'd seen around the apartment complex ran through the parking lot. They were chasing a dog, a squat black mutt with brown ears. There was an arrow through the dog's hind leg.

"Well," Quincy said, "the night's already weird." He turned the music up and started the car. "Clear on your side?" he asked. I nodded that it was and he eased the car out of the lot.

We drove for a long time. Quincy played both sides of several tapes and sang along with them. "You're a good singer," I said, but

Quincy just laughed. Finally we turned onto a canal bank and parked alongside a stand of towering eucalyptus trees. It was a bright night. It seemed I could see the Sierras sprouting up out of the horizon. Quincy got out and took something from the trunk, then he walked off into the woods. It gave me a sick feeling in my stomach to see him disappear like that.

"Come on," he shouted.

I blew on the glass again, then once more. Though there was no trace of the word, I couldn't stop thinking about it.

"You coming?" Quincy called out.

I followed his crunching footsteps through the trees. After a short walk through the dark we reached the lip of a moonlit swale where lush, dewy grass angled downward and flattened out into a square field. The ground was thick with grass — real grass, like in a back yard, not field grass or crabgrass or Johnson grass. The banks were tree-lined and contained the blue moonlight like water in a swimming pool. It was beautiful. There were golf balls everywhere.

I slid down the grassy slope on my backside. The smell of the field rushed through me, and when I stood up, cool grass sifted into my underwear. Quincy sidestepped down the bank after me. He had something in his hand. It looked like a cardboard tube from Christmas wrap.

"Toss me one," he said. He hoisted the tube to his shoulder in the pose of a batter.

"What is that?" I asked.

"Jack handle," Quincy said. "It's real light, though. I think it's for girls." Though I said nothing, Quincy quickly added, "It was with the car when I bought it."

I picked up a golf ball and threw it. Quincy swung the jack

handle. He missed, but what a swing — all arms and elbows and bared teeth. I imagined I felt the wind from it.

"Throw another," he said.

I threw another.

Again Quincy whiffed. "Goddamnit!" he said. He slammed the handle into the ground.

"Didn't you play sports or anything when you were a kid?" I asked him.

"Naw. We lived in the woods. Mostly we just worked and shot stuff. Kids in town played the sports."

"What did you shoot?" I asked.

"Birds and squirrels and fish. Mostly birds."

"It doesn't seem like you'd shoot things," I said. "Animals, I mean."

"Why not?"

"I don't know."

"Tell me. Why not?"

"I don't know. I guess because you wouldn't let me have a beer."

"That don't mean I can't be a killer too," Quincy said.

"Okay," I said. "Sorry."

"You think I ain't?"

"What?"

"A killer."

"Yeah," I said. "You are."

"Well I *can* be," Quincy said. "Don't you worry about that."

"I won't," I said.

Quincy flipped the handle to me. It *was* light — aluminum, maybe. I swung it almost without effort. "Pitch one to me," I said. I took up my new pigeon-toed stance and held the bat high. Quincy tossed over a golf ball and when I swung, the ball exploded off the jack handle and sailed high into the eucalyptus. Something like electricity ran through me.

"Shit fire," Quincy said. He threw another one and again I spanked it into the night. He pitched ball after ball, and each one I ripped into the trees like Reggie Jackson.

"I'm killing it," I said.

"You are," Quincy said. "I'm seeing it."

Quincy got tired of pitching before I got tired of hitting. He threw a ball straight up and watched it arc and fall back to the ground. He looked up at the sky. "Your daddy, was he in the navy? Is that how you all ended up here?"

"No," I said. "He was a cook. He got a job at the high school. The Kings County Regional Occupational Program. That's what it was called. He taught kids how to cook and do restaurant stuff, except after a year the program was cut. They figured people could get jobs at Denny's without my dad's help."

"I like Denny's," Quincy said.

"That's where my dad met my mom. She had this boyfriend we lived with, Douglas. He got drunk and smashed her in the face while she was working. My dad saw the whole thing from the kitchen."

"What did he do?" Quincy asked.

I was ashamed to say, but it seemed like Quincy of all people would understand. "Nothing," I said.

Quincy nodded.

"Her nose was broken," I said. "She had to quit her job because of missing so much work from it. Douglas paid all the rent and bills and stuff for a while."

"Your daddy didn't do nothing, huh?"

"He talked to her on the phone a lot when Douglas was at work.

Finally he moved with us here to get her away from him. He got that job and we rented a house by Tommy."

"That sounds real nice," Quincy said.

"Yeah," I said. "I never lived in a house before."

"What did you live in?"

"Apartments."

Quincy grinned. "Were they metal?"

"No," I said. "Our house was green, though."

I gave Quincy back the jack handle and pitched another ball to him. "Watch it all the way in," I said. He took the same wild swing, and when he missed again he threw the handle and kicked a golf ball halfway up the bank. I shagged the jack handle and brought it back to him. "Like this," I said. I positioned the handle in his hands. I pushed my hand into his back to straighten his stance. "Feet together," I said. He moved one foot, but not enough, so I kicked his boot toward the other one until he was squared up. "Right shoulder up more," I said. "And don't swing for the moon." He just stared at me, his face a blank. I pushed up on his shoulder until he was upright instead of leaning back. "Flatten your swing plane," I said. I stood like a batter and demonstrated. "Level," I said.

"Level," Quincy repeated.

"Yeah, level."

Quincy fanned on the first three pitches, but on the fourth the ball clicked off the jack handle and ripped through the air like it was shot from a gun. "Hoooweee!" Quincy howled. "How 'bout that!" He flung the handle away and took off on a long slow trot around imaginary bases. I dropped down in the grass and cheered him on.

After his lap, Quincy came and sat on the ground next to me. He was winded. He winked at me. "What do you think?" he asked. He put his hand on the top of my head like I was a jar of mayonnaise. It was a heavy and unnatural weight, and I quickly ducked away from it. I stood up and began to gather golf balls.

"That didn't mean nothing," Quincy said.

"I know," I said. I picked up the jack handle. "I just feel like batting some more."

Quincy sat in the grass and said nothing. Then he said, "Why'd you jump back like that?"

"I didn't."

"The hell you didn't," he said. He got up and grabbed the jack handle away from me. "You don't know nothing," he said.

I stepped back from him. "Leave me alone," I said.

Quincy winced. He covered his face with his hand. "Leave you alone?" he said. His voice was different now. Sad.

Leave me alone. That wasn't it, exactly. *Thank you* — maybe that was right. It seemed like I should know, but I didn't. Like Quincy said — I didn't know nothing. And it hurt, somewhere down deep. I didn't know how to erase pain, and I didn't know yet that it wasn't something I could teach myself, like mental discipline or pigeon toes.

I moved toward Quincy and the rock in my shoe bit sharply into my heel. I turned my toes inward, took a few steps, then stopped. The woods were pink with first light, and Quincy was staring out at them, at the spot where his home run had disappeared.

"Sorry," I said.

Quincy nodded but said nothing, just kept watching something

I couldn't see, maybe whatever pictures came with the music I hadn't been able to hear. Then from the far end of the field a noise like shuffling leaves broke the quiet. It was a possum, stumbling like a drunk out of the trees. When it got to the edge of the basin it didn't stop, but went blindly forward until it lost balance and tumbled end over end down the grassy embankment. When it hit bottom, it lay stunned for a moment in the grass then struggled to its feet. It stood there, big as a country mailbox and mint white but for the black tips of its fur, and it waited a few seconds as if clearing its head. Then it headed toward us with alarming speed and dexterity.

"I'm ready to go," I said.

"He's rabid," Quincy said.

I hollered out to shoo the possum away, but he kept coming. I threw a golf ball and nearly pegged him. I threw another, and another. "He's sleepwalking," I said.

"He ain't," Quincy said. "He's a walking bag of poison is what he is." I kept throwing balls until finally I hit the animal square in the head. It stopped for a second, stunned, then continued forward. "Wake up!" I shouted.

"Stay back," Quincy said.

"Let's get out of here."

Quincy looked at me for a long time. "Scared?" he asked.

I felt the stab of the rock in my heel. "No," I said. "I'm just sick of this place. I'm ready to leave."

"Well I ain't."

I turned to walk off but he took me by the neck, like Tommy had earlier, only with soft hands, and pointed me toward the possum. It was almost right in front of us now. "You should be afraid," Quincy said. When the animal got to us, Quincy lifted a boot and gave him a rap on the nose. The possum stopped. Its eyes were black and vacant. Quincy let loose of me and I backed away. He reached out with the jack handle and gave the possum a light whack on the head. "You sick?" he asked it. Then to me he said, "It's gonna die, you know. It could still do some damage." He raised the handle a few feet above the possum's head and let it fall. The animal staggered but remained upright. It moved quickly toward Quincy and we both jumped back. But then it stopped, like it was waiting on us to do something.

"Let's just leave," I said again, only this time my voice was plaintive instead of tough, and when Quincy answered me, his was too.

"I ain't *ready* to leave," he said. "I *can't*."

He got into the batter's stance I showed him and swung the jack handle toward the ground. He meant to stop it before it hit the possum, I know he did, like a check swing. I could tell because his arms snapped taut right at the end — he couldn't go through with it. But the momentum of the swing was too much. The handle hit the possum's head with a sharp crack and Quincy looked at me like a little boy who'd snapped off the short end of a wishbone.

The possum teetered for an instant, then fell onto its side. It labored to stand but could only lay and kick at the air like a wind-up toy.

Quincy jerked me back by the shirt when I knelt down beside the possum. "You crazy?" he said. He watched me for a few seconds — I didn't say or do anything — then he lifted his leg and pinned the animal's head to the ground with his boot. He squatted down and held the possum by the scruff of the neck. "Go on," he said.

"Go on what?"

"I don't know. Whatever you was gonna do before I grabbed you, I guess."

I moved a little closer, scared now. The possum didn't seem to notice me. I bent down next to Quincy and sunk my fingers into its fur. It was coarse and stiff, not soft the way it looked. And it was thick too. I stroked up and down its back and sides, brushing my fingernails against its skin, feeling the rise and fall of every breath. I felt its tail. It was bony, and the short hair only rubbed one way, like the lint brush my dad had used every morning on his one teaching suit. My dad wore a suit while teaching kids how to flip eggs in a frying pan with just a flip of the wrist. God, I missed him.

"Hold him tight," I said.

"What are you gonna do?"

"Just hold him," I said.

Quincy tightened his grip on the scruff. I took the possum by the middle and stood him up. Then I let go. He toppled over and fell free of Quincy's grasp. We both fell backward and Quincy pulled me quickly away. My legs were covered with wet grass.

"He *is* gonna die," Quincy said.

"Yeah."

Quincy picked up the jack handle and gave me a light pop on the arm with it. He tossed me the keys to his car. "Get it warmed up for me," he said. "And find that song I like."

I went back to the car but I waited for Quincy in the passenger seat. I wasn't ready to be starting cars yet.

We didn't say much as we drove back to town. Quincy kept the music loud. It was still foreign to me — nothing I could feel past my ears — but then Quincy sang again, and that I felt. I kicked off my shoe and tossed the pebble out the window.

We were still a ways from my apartment when Quincy stopped the car. "Better get out here," he said. His gaze was distant and wan. He looked peaceful, like the possum as it marched toward us.

"See you sometime," I said.

"I don't know," Quincy said. "Maybe."

"Yeah. Maybe."

I got out and watched Quincy's big white car float off like a cloud. The navy base was to the west about ten miles. Quincy was heading east.

When I opened the door to my apartment, Stan was naked at the refrigerator, drinking down an RC. "Ain't you been here all night?" he asked.

"I was out," I said.

"Out where?"

"What do you care?" I said.

"I don't, really," Stan said. "But I guess since me and your mom's getting married I got to act like I do. And I guess you better knock off with that smart-mouthing from now on too."

"She's not marrying you," I said.

Stan grinned. "You're giving her away," he said. "She thought that'd be cute."

As Stan drank off the last of his soda, I felt the hollow growing in my stomach. It grew and grew until it was all I felt, and I realized I hadn't eaten all night. I reached into my pocket and touched the two dollars my mom had left me for dinner. "I'm not giving anyone away," I said.

Stan slung his arm around my shoulder and with his dangling hand he grabbed my nipple through my shirt and gave it a pinch. "Come on now," he said. "Give us a yes."

Stan was laughing as I ducked away. "Don't be a pussy," he said.

"I'm not a pussy," I said. Then, as if to no one in particular, or maybe to myself, I said something else, something loud and strong that felt like music swishing around in my empty innards. I said, "Jarhead."

The inside part of the Snow Queen was dark, and I realized it was still early morning. I sat on the picnic table for a few minutes and waited. Then I saw Werner moving around inside so I rapped on the little glass window. When he slid it open, a blast of cool, greasy air blew my hair back. "Not yet open," he said. "Two hours more."

"A hamburger," I said. "And small fries and a small root beer." I held out my two dollars.

Werner looked at me, and his brow did a funny quivering thing. He shut the window and disappeared into the kitchen. I didn't know if he was going to come back or not. I sat on the table again and waited. After a long time Werner came back. He opened the window and handed me a tray loaded down with the three-dollar Big Bargain. He accepted my two. "You look hungry," he said. There was a rack of Swiss chocolates in the window. Werner liked that he was from Switzerland and not from here. He took a triangular Toblerone chocolate bar from the rack and put it on my tray.

I thanked him. He nodded and slid the window shut. He smiled again through the glass. Again he nodded. He opened the window. "I forgot something?" he asked.

I shook my head.

Werner reached his arm through the window and gently pushed me back from the counter. He was still smiling. "You're welcome already," he said.

family sports

I'M AT THE five-dollar blackjack table when the pit supervisor comes up behind me and slides something into the pocket of my dealer's smock. "Message," he says. "Call home." All at once it feels like I'm dealing bricks. After an earthquake once, my father told people that I'd warned him it was coming. "As soon as I heard those runaway hiccups," he'd said, "I got Judy and the girls into the doorway. You can keep the barnyard animals. I'll keep Claire." In part, he was trying to bestow on me a talent to keep me up with my older sister, Camille. But I'm sure part of him believed it too. I was a sensitive child. Nearly everything said in our house, every side-long glance, was layered with hidden meaning. It was all clear to me though. The pressure between tectonic plates, to a young girl, feels like a shift in the movement of her own small world.

They called me nervous. Anxious. Really I was just quiet, which is all you can be when you know certain things. But now I am grown, my own person of sorts, and this slip of paper in my pocket, even mention of the word "home," has me in knots. I know my father is dead.

The guy on my left, serious in a slick gray suit, a computer salesman, maybe an insurance fraud investigator, slaps the table for another card. He looks me in the eye for the first time tonight. "Card," he says. He's the kind that comes to Reno instead of Tahoe because the odds are like a jillionth of a percent better. People who care where they are generally go to Tahoe.

"I have a six up," I remind him, an almost guaranteed loser. He's showing a face card.

"See this pile of chips?" he says. "There's exactly four hundred and sixty-four dollars there. Want to count it?"

I turn over his card — a four. Then I hand out a flurry of little numbers to the other players and bust myself with a jack.

When my relief steps in I automatically give the table two neat raps so the eye in the sky and anyone else watching knows I'm pocketing my measly tips and not a stack of hundreds.

In the casino's bathroom, which is bigger than my whole apartment, I unfold the note. "Call your father."

Mom picks up after the first ring. "He's just overreacting," she whispers. "Go back to work, honey. He shouldn't have bothered you."

"Then why did he?" I ask.

The line clicks and Daddy comes on. He's probably on the extension in the garage. Mom banned smoking in the house when she started selling silk flowers a few years ago ("I can't take them into peoples' houses stinking of smoke"), and since then Daddy has taken up smoking full-time. He has emphysema at least; I don't let myself think beyond that.

"Claire?"

"Daddy, what did you call me for? You scared the crap out of me."

"Sounds like a guilty conscience, girlie. Thought I was dead, huh?"

"Claire's working," Mom says.

"Judy, get off the damn line. Claire called *me*."

"How can you be so cruel?" Mom asks, then she hangs up her line.

"Your mother needs you to come home," Daddy says.

"What's wrong?"

"I'll tell you when you're home. When can you come?"

"Every time I come home you talk about your will. Do whatever you want. Don't tell me."

"Your mother's been arrested," Daddy says. He coughs, more than a little theatrically. "We're trying to keep her out of jail, but . . ."

"Arrested?"

"Shoplifting. And you're goddamn right I'm redoing the will. What do you expect?"

I try to picture it: Mom, jail, bad manners. Women with rotting teeth and no makeup urinating in view of each other.

"They don't put women Mom's age in jail, Daddy. They'll just give her a fine or something."

"They did that. The first three times. Everyone I knew at the department's gone. I think she's going in."

Andres is in the middle of his routine with a Long Island iced tea when I stop by the casino lounge to tell him I'm going back to Fresno. He tightens the blending canister onto the glass, holds it behind his ear like a quarterback in the old Statue of Liberty play, then lets it slide down the groove of his back into his other hand. I whistle, more of a wolf whistle really, and he winks at me like he's caught me spying. I suppose he has. He places the drink in front of a woman wearing a full-length evening gown with no back to speak of though it's two in the afternoon. She slides Andres a ten and waves off the change. She slips her feet out of her fuck-me pumps and rubs them along the bar's padded footrest. "Mm," she sighs, sipping on her drink.

Andres meets me at our end of the bar with a Diet Pepsi. The woman in the dress watches his ass when he walks. He turns, looks back, and hams for her.

"Having fun?" I ask.

"All part of the game," he says, flashing his big tip. He's right. I'd make more money if I played the game the way Andres does, but I like winning too much. People don't tip winning dealers.

"I have to go to my parents' for a few days," I tell Andres. "I think my mom's sick."

He places his hand on mine. "What's wrong with her?"

"Or maybe my dad," I say. "I'm not sure."

Andres looks at me off-balance, the way I like him. "Who's sick?"

"I just got this call and I have to go. I'm flying."

"Do you mind if I stay at your apartment?" he says. "My little brother's friends are in town. They act like they're in Tijuana." Andres's lips curl around the whispery *j* like a blown kiss. *Tijuana.*

The woman down the bar calls out to him. "Andres." He pretends not to notice.

"I was going to ask anyway," he says.

Andres and I have been together for two months. We agreed to keep things light. No expectations, no disappointments. But I really want him in my apartment. He is exactly what my apartment needs.

"Andres," the woman calls.

Andres ignores her. "When are you coming back?" he says.

"Don't know. I'll just show up, I guess."

"How will I know when?"

"Why would you need to know? Planning on company?"

"Maybe," he says. "Or maybe I want something to look forward to."

"Smooth."

The woman at the bar is insistent now. "Andres!"

"How about one for the road?" Andres says.

I nod, aware only vaguely of what I'm agreeing to but agreeable nevertheless. Andres pours me a tequila shot and without hesitation I take it down. He gives me a lemon wedge and I sink my teeth into it hungrily. Neither the liquor nor the lemon startles my mouth anymore. Andres leans across the bar and kisses me.

"That doesn't prove anything," I say.

Camille is waiting when the plane lands. She looks pretty good, wearing what might be her natural weight if she's still got one. We hug the proper length of time and she asks about my flight. I'm fine. Work's fine. Yes, I'm still dealing blackjack. No, the management opportunities don't look too good.

"I'm sorry you have to come home under these circumstances," Camille says. "Mom would have been here but she's in court. She didn't want us there."

"Will she be coming home?"

"Of course. Don't be so dramatic." Camille takes my carryon and waits for me to walk ahead of her. "Dad's waiting in the car."

"I hope nobody parked close."

"You don't need to say that," Camille says.

Daddy is like a Venus flytrap with strangers. He projects a natural enthusiasm for their lives, and they repay that rare kindness with their secrets. I used to leave him in the car while I'd run into a store for nylons or milk and when I came out he'd have some housewife with penciled-on eyebrows talking about radical mastectomies and income tax evasion. But any commiseration these people feel from my father is artificial, the residue of thirty years questioning victims about crimes too frivolous for duty cops. Daddy was a real policeman, card-carrying and all, but he did his work over the phone, calling the nearly bruised and quickly offended, taking the details. He worked at it all the time, day and night, on the clock and off. Most of it he did from home. "How many hookers did you actually see peeing on your lawn?" I heard him ask once. He held his hand over the mouthpiece and laughed to beat the band, but when he removed his hand to speak, his voice was pure honey, sweet enough to talk a perfect stranger out of something as precious as anger. Now his throat and lungs are fried from smoking and he sounds like a disposal full of spoons. No matter what anyone says, he won't see a doctor.

"Doesn't the airport look great?" Camille says. She points out the new water fountain and brushed aluminum facade as we approach the main terminal. "They're spending eight million dollars renovating it. It's supposed to be finished in the fall."

"What's the point?" I ask.

Camille sighs. "Does there *have* to be a point? Is it so terrible that Fresno should have a nice airport?"

It's not terrible, it just isn't honest. The old airport looked like Fresno: sprawling, functional, no frills. It's beside the point to Camille that airports, along with bedrooms, are the center of everything: You're either losing someone there or getting them back. She wants a fountain in the background.

"Mom's dealing with everything very well," Camille says. "But let's let them bring it up, okay?" She looks at me calmly, point-blank. She puts a hand on my shoulder. "We'll get through this!" She guides me onto the electric sidewalk. Sister Supportive of the Eating Disorder. She pinches some airplane fuzz from my sweater. "This is a cute top."

Daddy says Camille's problems started early — Sudden Infant Emergence Syndrome. As a girl, she used to hold me down and fart on my clenched lips. She got her period young. When it came she danced around our bedroom and waved her soiled napkin like Old Glory before marrying it to my neck. We were sisters. I chased her around the room trying to touch it to her while Daddy banged on the door. "What's going on in there?" he wanted to know. Emboldened by her new right to privacy, Camille opened the door, pointed right at him, and shouted, "Get out!" Daddy muttered something and shuffled back to the telephone. When Camille was asleep, I felt around in the dark until I found a napkin, the startling new object of our game. I affixed it to my pajama bottoms and lay there in the dark pretending it was mine.

Many years later, Camille, a law student, had bouts of anorexia and depression. Every downward movement of the scale tightened the skin on the family drum, and in the good old Mortensen tradition we explained it away — School Is Hard — and talked about something else. Our parents were having their worst marital problems to date. When Camille got down to eighty pounds, Mom and Dad announced, in a remarkable family meeting, that the wrinkles in their marriage could be ironed out (Mom's words). Mom crushed Camille in her arms and Daddy, not sure what to do, shook my hand.

By the time Camille finished law school she was married and

weighed over two hundred pounds. In five years she bought, decorated, and sold three new houses, each much grander than the last, and gave her husband three slow-eyed children to answer to his family names: Buster, Hickey (a girl!), and Jasper. I tell myself at Christmas and on birthdays that I love these children, that they are not their mother, but in truth I am indifferent to them. Camille is a TV mother now, a housewife extraordinaire. Turn that frown upside down, lemons to lemonade, all that shit. She never even took the bar. I think Daddy might actually hate her.

"So things are going to change," Daddy concludes, his voice raspy, depleted. "Can't have a loony in the house and keep things the same."

Except for the part about jail and bail and loony bins there wasn't much we hadn't heard before. Daddy likes telling the story. He likes the thought of Mom being nuts because it vindicates him for thirty years of her petty judgments against him.

The speech has been over for just minutes when Mom bursts through the door. She hugs me and hugs me and wants to fix us all lunch though it's almost time for dinner. "You're so skinny," she tells me. She looks as though she might cry.

"How much time did they give you?" Daddy asks her.

"I hope you haven't been listening to him," my mother says to me. "He's exaggerating, I'm sure." She buzzes through the living room and tidies what's already tidy.

Daddy kicks out the footrest of the La-Z-Boy and settles in. "Are you going to tell us what happened or not?" he asks.

"Can't I sit with Claire for two minutes and visit?" Mom says. "I don't want to spoil her trip talking about me."

"I came to have my trip spoiled, Mom. What happened?"

"Later," she says. She takes my hand and strokes it like a swatch of carpet. "I want to hear about you."

I take the hand back. "Mom!"

Her smile sags at the corners. She gets up and opens the refrigerator. She flips open all the compartments, slides out all the drawers. She troops out a bunch of food — carrots, bacon, a lemon, a tube of cookie dough, a half-eaten bowl of Jell-O, baking soda — and puts it on the counter. Then she stands back and looks at it. Her shoulders begin to shake. I should go to her, I know. But I can't. All that food on the counter. I can't go near it. My stomach feels like a bag of snakes.

The footrest of Daddy's La-Z-Boy slams down. "What happened, Judy, goddamnit?"

"Please!" Mom says. Her cheeks are trembling, her thumbs worrying the fine fabric of her skirt. "It's *private*, can't you understand? It's *my* business."

"It's a matter of public record," Dad says.

Mom leaves me and this food in the kitchen and takes a seat on the couch. Camille is quickly beside her. She puts a hand on our mother's knee. "It's a cry for help, Mom. A symptom that something else is wrong. I know that better than anyone."

Fucking Camille. By next month she'll be pregnant or have a new house or be fifty pounds fatter, and she wants to help.

Mom pushes her hand away and stands up. "I don't want to be helped," she says. "If you want to help someone, help your father finish that effing will." She disappears down the dark hallway lined with photos of everyone smiling.

"I like working on it," Daddy shouts after her. "It reminds me of what's important."

Mom reemerges for a second, an unexpected jewel handed her. "It makes you *forget* about what's important," she says.

Camille turns a glare on me. "What are you laughing at?"

"'Effing'?" I laugh. "You think she even means 'fucking'?"

"You're ill," Camille says. She kneels on the floor beside Daddy's chair. "Daddy," she says, "let's be constructive, okay?"

Daddy looks at her frankly and without affection. "I don't *need* any help with my will," he says. "And if I did I'd get a real lawyer."

Camille drops his hand and stands over him. "You're just lashing out," she says. "I don't think I can bring your grandchildren around anymore if you two can't get along."

"Your breath could knock a buzzard off a shit wagon," Daddy says. "Go stand somewhere else."

Camille collects her purse and leaves without a word.

Daddy winks at me. Teammates.

As Daddy sleeps through the afternoon in his chair, I amble through the house wondering which things Mom got at a five-finger discount. What would she be likely to steal? Knickknacks? Things that fit nicely into the pocket? Not food, I hope. In her bedroom I fondle the sentimental treasures of my youth, items once too valuable or personal for me to touch. At what point in her life, I wonder, did she start stealing? Was she my age? How many lifted items does this dresser alone hide? The tiny lead alligator with green glass eyes now looks stolen. So does the atomizer half full of the blue perfume. And earrings! A cache of them, four or five pairs, still attached to backboards. The styles are so different, selected by the hand, perhaps, independent of the preoccupied eye. How bold would my mother be in her pilfering? A large item would be too proud, but a valuable one too malicious. Something cheap, though, less than a few dollars, doesn't seem worth the trouble. I know that's not why she does it, but I still hate to think of her stealing something even a body in need would scoff at. I guess I'm a larceny snob.

It doesn't make sense. It's like there's this whole other person inside my mother that I've never seen, one my father only catches glimpses of and chalks up to lunacy. I'm ashamed to think it, but I wonder if I'd like that person more than the one I know now.

It wasn't always this way between Mom and Daddy. I remember them playing duets on the piano and singing two-part harmony while Camille and I drummed on the couch with wooden spoons. I was little, but I remember it. Then that sort of play just stopped. There was no more piano, no more all of us together except on holidays so Mom could bring out her Christmas china or Thanksgiving china or Fourth of July china. Mom must have believed, like so many women, that the sacrifice of her own fulfillment for ours would be worth it in the end. But somewhere along the way she forgot that this isn't her, isn't anybody. Maybe she's only stealing back what she lost.

The bedroom light snaps on, and suddenly I'm aware of my hand in my mother's bureau drawer. "I was just looking . . ." I hold up the silver powder box. "These things from when I was little . . . see . . ." Mom steps around the bed, takes the evidence from my hand and places it back in the drawer. She slips the drawer shut and winks at me as if we're conspiring to keep a secret.

"I'm sorry," I tell her. "I didn't mean to snoop. I mean, I wasn't snooping."

She goes into her small bathroom. "Your sister seems happy to have you here," she says. "You two haven't seen each other in a while. Doesn't she look good?"

"I suppose."

"She looks fine," Mom says. "But you're so thin. I wish —"

"Forget about how we look, Mom. Talk to me."

"Remember how we used to keep two boxes inside for firewood, and you and Camille would race to fill them up and the first one to get hers full had to brush the other one's hair, and you'd sit in front of the fire and brush and brush and then the other one would brush and brush? How you'd throw the brushed-out hair into the fire and it would sizzle and drift up the chimney and you thought that was so wonderful? I think about that."

"Oh God."

"What?" Mom asks. "What's wrong?"

"Nothing," I say. "Nothing. I just thought of something but it's okay." What I thought of is: We don't have a fireplace, have never had one. "Oh God," I say, only quietly, and this time to myself.

"Mom," I say, "I want to tell you I think it's okay, what you did. I know it's important for you to have everything hunky-dory, but taking a risk like that, it kind of lets us know it's not. I respect that. I think Daddy should understand more."

"I don't know what you're talking about," Mom says.

"You know," I say. "The stealing. I'm saying maybe you're stealing to get to Daddy."

I get up and peek in at her. She is sitting on the toilet lid staring blankly into the mirror. "Change of life," she says. "That's all it is." Her voice reverberates off the gleaming skin of the room, the white tile, the twin basins, the chromium trim on the glass. Everything is polished to a supernatural shine, a room dipped in glass. I duck out quickly and curl up on her bed.

In a moment she is beside me on the bed. "I'm tired," she says. Together we lay there caressed by the silence, watching the evening shadows climb the wall.

"It's okay," I say. "I understand."

"You understand," she says flatly. "Oh good."

Soon the room is dark.

"Do you know who you remind me of?" Mom asks.

"Who?"

"Me," she says. "I know that probably sounds like an insult to you. I just mean that it's a mistake to think you can ever know someone completely. Even yourself."

I tuck myself into the crook of my mom's tiny arm. "It's cold in here," I say. She puts her arms around my shoulders, covering more of me than I would have thought possible. She smoothes my hair with soft, steady strokes. Soon she is shaking again, this time with sleep tremors. She begins snoring loudly. I am freezing. In the dark silence I whisper, "This used to be the warmest room in the house."

Mom got forty hours of community service washing city buses. When she finally tells us it seems like a mistake. I picture her with a limp garden hose squirting a blimp-size mud-sopped bus. Then I remember an essay from high school about a boy in a Catholic school who was punished by a nun for some juvenile foolishness. His punishment was to spend the afternoon at the head of the class standing in a garbage can.

"They're trying to humiliate you, Mom!"

"Who?" Daddy asks.

"The fucking court," I say. "What can Mom do to a bus?"

Daddy zaps the TV on and settles into his chair. "Steal it, maybe."

"Don't underestimate me," Mom chimes.

Daddy flips through the channels until he finds one of those tabloid TV shows. Real crime, cops on patrol, that stuff. He points to a man on the screen with a bloodied face. "She got off light," he says.

By her third day of bus-washing duty, Mom's wondering why I'm still here. She keeps waking me up before she leaves in the morning to ask if she should take something out for dinner. I tell her she can if she wants, and I see from her look that I'm not really answering her question. The truth is, I don't know exactly why I'm still here. Andres is living in my apartment without me. I told Mom and Daddy that I took a leave of absence from work and it didn't matter when I went back. That, by now, is no lie. It's just that I feel those same inner rumblings Daddy says I used to feel, like an earthquake is coming.

I dial my number in Reno and on about the twentieth ring Andres picks up. He's breathing heavily. "What!" he shouts.

"Nothing," I scream. The plastic casing of the handset shatters as I slam it down.

At dinner, Dad asks Mom to steal them a new phone.

I'm with my sister at McDonald's. Jasper, the baby, sits without movement or expression in Camille's lap. He's an odd thing — long as my leg already, flat dark hair, far-apart eyes. More like a small man than an infant. A glazed-over look clouds his face. My other nephew and niece are sharing the table next to us with three children from Camille's neighborhood. Camille has a minivan and runs an unlicensed daycare. She gets twelve hundred dollars a month, she told me, for keeping these three until late afternoon. Their mother has made them lunches in paper bags. Egg salad sandwiches, it looks like. The children have unwrapped the sandwiches from the plastic but aren't eating. Camille's two have been screaming all morning for Happy Meals. *We're starving! You want us to die! We hate you, Mommy.* Now they're too busy with the toys from their Happy Meals to eat. Of the other three children, the two oldest are boys, the youngest a girl. The girl says to Hickey, Camille's girl, "Can I have a French fry?"

Hickey pushes the limp pouch of fries at her. "I don't care," she says. The little girl eats one. She looks at her brother and he eats one. She slides a fry over to her other brother but he pushes it away. He takes a huge bite of his egg sandwich and chomps it with his mouth open wide, looking at Camille.

"He called you because you're their daughter," Camille says.

"What do they expect me to do?"

"To be there for Mom."

"What does that *mean?* Mom doesn't even want me there."

"Camille," says the boy who took a French fry. "Buster's not eating his hamburger. Can I have it?"

"Buster," Camille says. "Are you going to eat your hamburger?"

"It's got pickles on it," Buster says. He too has dark hair like his father, but his face is pure Camille. The eyes, yes, but mostly the fire behind them.

"Pickles come off," Camille says.

Buster sighs, pushes the burger over to the nice boy then pokes his finger through the bun. The boy turns quickly to Camille.

"It's not important what you do," Camille says. "Just be there for them. They're your parents, for God's sake."

"They're yours too. You're here, what do they need me for?"

Camille looks up from her McSomething Salad. She says, "I can't believe you. I kept them together once, if you remember. It almost killed me."

"Maybe you shouldn't have."

Camille props the baby up on the seat beside her. She pushes her plastic tray aside, wipes the table. "Come on, kids," she says. "Hurry up." The baby watches my sister like she's a stranger, not his mother at all, or even someone he knows. He jerks his thumb into his eye and starts crying. It's like the sound from a goat. She brings the baby to her and shushes him with whispers to the top of his head. She looks up at me with this smug, satisfied smile, like she'd just invented the computer chip or something. "You don't understand the first thing about family," she says.

Whatever brief soothing effect my presence had on my parents is over. Daddy is out of control with self-righteousness, and the pretense of household peace is wearing on Mom's nerves. I can't raise Andres on the phone.

Feeling anxious, caged, I go into Daddy's study to find a book. He follows me. "What are you after?" he says.

"Something to read. Don't worry, I'm not going to boot up your will and leave myself the house."

He leaves me alone, but I hear him pacing in the hallway like a spooked horse. I scan the bookshelves for something written in the last twenty years but there's nothing. Suddenly I feel comforted to find the same titles I grew up ignoring — the collection of Reader's Digest condensed classics, *The Guinness Book of Records*, *Chariots of the Gods*, *The Rise and Fall of the Third Reich*, every book about Watergate ever written. For some reason this makes me think about how little I've seen of the world. California, Nevada, the Grand Canyon.

I decide on an encyclopedia. As I lift the door to the lawyer's bookcase where the World Books have been kept since before I was born, Madonna's metal-jacketed nudie book, *Sex*, catches the sun's glint. The word *Slut* announces itself from a second title. Then I look closely and see that it's a videotape. They're all videotapes. *The Honeymoaners. Hot Tuna Sandwich.* I quietly close the cabinet door.

"Hurry up in there," Daddy yells from the other room. The percussion in his throat makes him sound a hundred miles away. "I've got work to do," he says.

I know I should look in the closet now because a voice telling me not to rages in my head. So I do it, I look. I open the door and sweep back the coats and there they are, a thousand more tapes, piles of magazines. I shut the closet door and grab an old *Consumer Reports* from a cardboard box. Daddy appears in the doorway, his face a twist of sick fear.

"Why did you call me here, Daddy?"

"Because Mom needs your help. Why? What do you think?"

"Do you love Mom?"

Suddenly Dad's eyes turn soft. "Do I love her?" he says. He unsnaps the clasp on his watch and spins it around and around on his wrist. He looks at the time, spins the band once more, twice, then looks again. "Of course I do," he says. "How else could I stand to be around her?"

"I don't know. By leaving each other alone, maybe."

"Princess," Daddy says, "that's the whole deal. Your mom and I are too old to be left alone."

"But what can *I* do?"

Daddy shakes his head. "I don't know, girlie," he says, his eyes hopeful. "What *can* you do?"

I'm reading *Consumer Reports*. Old men in white lab coats test-driving stand mixers. The science of consumerism. No ads. "Why does Daddy still get this?" I ask Mom. "He hasn't bought anything in ten years."

Mom's lying back in her chair, her little feet propped on a little embroidered stool. Her eyes are closed but her glasses aren't yet parked in her hair. "He likes to know how much things are worth," she says. "He worries about being cheated."

Daddy is rapt in *Unsolved Mysteries.* Tonight's installment is about a guy in Florida who's married to seventeen different women. One of them is learning that fact on camera. From his cadre of other wives, the reporter tells the woman, her husband stole tens of thousands of dollars. Cars are missing, artwork, jewelry. One woman was bilked out of a cowhide sofa. The reporter calls the man "the King of Hearts."

"When are you gonna be on one of these shows, Judy? Why don't you go on one and make me rich."

"Maybe I will," Mom says. "Maybe after you're dead I'll marry some con artist and give him all your money."

Daddy sits forward. "What makes you think you're getting any of my money?"

"Oh, I'm just ribbing you. Hush up."

"Kid all you want," Daddy says, "I'm serious. You're as loony as the day is long. You don't know your ass from five cents."

"In case you didn't notice your daughter sitting right here —"

"I'm glad she's here," he says. "About time someone else sees the kind of a goddamn nutbird I put up with every day."

"Jesus, Daddy, lay off."

"I'm just sitting here watching TV," Mom says. "Same as you."

Daddy turns to me with the shattered look of a lost child. "You're taking her side?" he says.

"I'm not taking anyone's side. Just leave me out of it."

"Fine," he says. "Wait till you see how left out of it you are." He gets up and heads for his study.

"That's enough," my mother says. "Stop right there. I'm sick of you holding that will over our heads. We don't want your stupid money. We don't want anything from you but peace. That's all you can give us anymore that means anything, so just stop all this." She is trembling.

Daddy stands above her now and studies her like an insect under glass. Instead of shrinking back or fixing a meal, Mom stares back at Daddy without apology and says, "Just be nice."

"Why don't you keep your little noises to yourself, Loony." He looks at me. "I ought to have her locked up for her own good. Take her down to the nutso ward and have her committed." His body slackens as he turns again to face Mom. Her expression is empty. He flaps his arms loosely at first, as if limbering up to run a race, but soon they are raised and he's waving them at his sides like some nightmarish sea bird hobbling into flight. His head lunges forward and back, forward and back.

"Daddy!"

His eyes widen. He swoops down at Mom and screeches. "Loo-loo-loo-loony! Loo-loo-loo-loony!"

"Daddy!"

He beats his wings faster, ferociously. "Loo-loo-loo-loony! Loo-loo-loo-loony!"

Mom doesn't appear to see him. She is looking past him at me.

When Daddy's noise stops, I feel the couch sink toward the center with his weight. My face is flushed and wet. I peek out from between my fingers and see his eyes, pinched and reddening, staring in at me. Mom is crying too now, great gulping sobs. They are both looking to me.

"What do you want from me?" I scream. "You want me to be like Camille and squeeze out a bunch of kids to hold over your heads? Well I can't. And I can't play this stupid game anymore, either."

"Sweetie," Daddy says. He reaches for me but I shrink away from him, dizzy, deceived, knowing there's only one thing I can do.

Andres and I once spent a whole night at the El Dorado playing the slots. We wandered in off the street to get warm. He dropped in a few nickels, then I did. The waitress came by and took our drink orders. We didn't have much money so we fed the machine slowly. Between plays we kissed and cooed, forgetting all about the cold waiting for us outside. Jacketed by bells and flashing lights, by old people rattling plastic buckets of nickels, we were in our own cocoon, the noise made soft by our inattention. Andres called up this sound in his throat, a soft, feathery flutter, like a pigeon. "That's the most wonderful thing I've ever heard," I said. Andres pulled back a little and asked if we were getting serious. I said no, then my mouth was on his again.

It was near daylight when we came out, the running lights of the marquee making their rounds against the purple desert morning. We weren't making much progress with car keys or zippers when we realized how drunk we were, how long we'd been with each other before time meant anything again.

I don't think we spent ten dollars.

From the pay phone at the Arco station I call the airline, then Andres at work. I tell him what time my plane will be landing that afternoon. "No games," I say. "Just show up if you want."

He apologizes for answering the phone the way he did before. "I was in the shower," he says. "It wouldn't stop ringing."

"It's okay," I tell him.

"I wasn't going to answer at all but it went on forever. It's not my apartment," he says.

I ask him to make the pigeon sound, that magical noise that drives away my chill. I listen for it, but all I hear is the noisy background of the casino.

"I couldn't hear it," I say.

"I'll do it again when you get home," he says. "Whenever you want."

I tell him not to make promises, not even little ones, just love me until you don't love me anymore. He laughs. He promises anyway. I press the phone to my cheek as he hangs up. Then I whisper after him, "I believe you."

separate states

DAD USED TO drive up and spend his nights at Shadow's apartment, but he had to stop because I was giving his stuff away. If he stayed gone a full night, I'd drive around the next day with items he particularly cherished — a handful of Snap-On wrenches, the ugly black Stetson he wore to bars — and give them to someone who looked like he might want them. No one ever turned me down. After a month or so of that, Dad sold my car. I came appropriately unglued, and he stayed home every night for a week. Then he spent a night at Shadow's. Fine. When he came home the next day nothing was gone, I didn't say a word. Then he spent two nights away. I put a sign on the bulletin board at the True Value: "Free — Brand New Stay-Rite pool pump and man's Citizen watch at . . ." The pool was clouding up nicely by the time Dad got home. He grounded me, but my generous nature grounded him right back.

So he took to the phone. You could bet that if he wasn't at work, he was lying in bed, fiber optically connected to his hideous scag mistress. Not being a veteran of the phone, though, he wasn't prepared for the bill that came — $1,200 for a single month. Shadow lives up in Fresno, not far, but still a long-distance call. "A phone ain't worth $1,200," Dad said, and let the bill go unpaid. He's no cheapskate by any means, in fact if anything he's the opposite — a sucker for a brand name, whatever the cost. But he wants a show for his dollar — maximum horsepower, a glossy finish, the most gadgetry and lines of resolution per inch. He likes the look on people's faces as they reconsider him in the flattering light of his purchases.

I love Dad and try to be patient with him, but when I picked up the phone and heard no tone, I went homicidal. "Does she have a 900 number?" I screamed. "Can't you find a woman in this whole area code?"

"What was I supposed to do?" he whined.

"Make *her* pay it."

"But she ain't got a pot to piss in," he said, "and I'm union." Then he blindly hit the rawest possible nerve. "No one ever calls you anyway."

I lined up his shot glasses from different states and crushed them one by one with the blender base as he watched. "If you ever speak to me again," I told him, "I'll sue you."

"Gonna be pretty quiet around here, I guess."

Rather than reconnect phone service, Dad decided to bring Shadow down to Hanford to live with us. I felt bad about giving his things away, breaking his jiggers — he *does* work hard — so I tried to be positive. "The phone savings can go toward my next car," I said.

Then I met Shadow. She was pale and sickly, gaunt and skinny as a switch. I didn't know what the word "ragamuffin" meant exactly but I'd heard it, and when I saw Shadow I understood. Holding on to the back pockets of her jeans were two tangly looking seaweed creatures, girls, silent and unsmiling. Nobody had said anything about kids.

"This is a real nice place," Shadow said to me. "You're a real lucky girl."

Pointing to Shadow's girls, I told Dad flatly, "They are *not* to use my bathroom."

"They won't," he said. "Now hush up."

Shadow inspected her new quarters, clearly pleased. Given Dad's personality, she probably expected something made of tin that ran just fine on leaded gas. "Welcome home," Dad said. He pulled Shadow full against him, beaming. She gave him a little squeeze around the pot and he about gacked his pants with pride. The thing I've never been able to abide in Dad is how grateful he is for so little affection. It's endearing for about a nanosecond, then you want to vomit.

"Don't expect me to entertain these waifs while you two are doing it," I said.

"What's with the mouth?" Shadow asked, whether of me or Dad I wasn't sure, but oooh, I had that bitch in my cross hairs. Then the bruises on her arms caught my eye, the needle marks, and for the first time in my life I was struck dumb. My brain was already packing a suitcase, picking out this top and those pants.

"Shadow," I said. "How are your T cells these days?"

Dad had had enough. "Why don't you haul your damn smart mouth to your room until you can act like a person."

"What's that supposed to mean?" Shadow asked. "My cells?"

Dad wilted visibly, meek and pathetic, terrified that I was going to wreck his grotesque abomination of a romance. Which I definitely was. "Erin," he begged. "C'mon."

"I just meant your health," I said then to Shadow. "You look tired."

Apropos of nothing in the known universe, Shadow said, "I fell down stairs last month and had some internal bleeding. I've got a tilted uterus."

I would have thrown up right there if I was my normal self. But as Shadow said "tilted uterus," something inside *me* shifted as well. I can't trace it for you and say, *That made me think of this, which reminded me of that, which clued me in on this other.* It doesn't work that way. Shadow just said those two words and I looked at Dad and saw a man who raised me from a baby and loved me and put up with all my shit, but who had no genetic claim on me, no blood connection at all. I realized then that my real father lived somewhere else. I saw the shape of his state in my mind, its lean finger pointing skyward, but I couldn't name it. Then, like a time snap, I heard Mom's voice: "Thank God I screwed around." It was a sideways crack she'd made when I was little, but the words didn't find me until the very day I'm describing. If you think it doesn't work that way, you're wrong.

Dad suddenly looked scared. "What's the matter?" he asked. "What's wrong with you?" My chest was tight, my breath coming shallow. He left Shadow's side and put his arm around me. I suppose I was crying by then. "You had a naked Norman," he said.

I nodded. "I saw my father's state," I said. "It's not our state. He's not you."

Dad pulled back from me a little and looked into my eyes, something he never did. He hugged me tight. "I love you, girlie," he said. He looked scared.

"Is something going on?" Shadow asked. "Should I leave?"

This is embarrassing to admit, but just then I left my father's —

this man's — arms, and steered Shadow by the shoulders into them. "Stay," I said. Like she was a dog.

When I was in kindergarten I up and left the playground one day without a word and walked home alone. The school called Dad at work and he rushed home in a panic to find me on the living room floor, asleep. "I slapped your face," he later told me, "but you were zonked." In my sleep, or maybe at school, I saw my Uncle Norman lying naked on his bathroom floor, unmoving. I woke up screaming, then I sobbed and sobbed, telling Daddy what I'd seen. He took me to my uncle's to show me that it was just my imagination — my overmation, he called it — that Norman was okay. He wasn't, though; he was dead. Naked on the bathroom floor. He'd had a fit and swallowed his tongue. More than once I'd seen him nearly die this way, seen Dad's fingers in his mouth, Uncle Norman's teeth clamped hard onto them, drawing blood.

After that day, Daddy was almost openly afraid of me. And I was afraid of myself.

I left Dad and Shadow like that, went to my room, and fell fast to sleep. It was night when I woke, the darkness chilling me inside and out. I didn't know quite where I was. A tingle, a fright ran through me. Then I lifted the handset of the phone and heard silence. I was home.

I slipped on some jeans and a sweater and walked down to the Beacon station to call my mother. She and Dad had always been separated, always.

"You whore!" I said when she answered. "You cheated on him. How could you?"

Mom yawned. "If you were married to Dodd, you'd know how easy it was."

My mother had a talent for the truth. She used it to quiet me, to cheat me out of my anger. It was a trick I'm sure Dad wished he knew.

Mom told me my real father's name. She told me what he looked like, what she sees of him in me. "Fire and wind and rain all at once," she said. "A walking natural disaster, just like you." Then she was quiet a minute. "But with him," she said, "it was just armor for a broken heart. I worry that your armor is really you."

She didn't apologize for that, she just went on, which is what Mom always did. "Your father didn't lay a finger on me," she told me. "All he cared about was our friendship, the way we were together, talking and laughing and telling the truth because I was married so friends was all we could be." She gave him plenty of chances, she said, but where other men would see opportunity, my father saw only her, and that she was hurting. "Things weren't very pretty with Dodd," she said. I asked how she got knocked up with me if this guy wouldn't touch her. "Because I'm a woman," she said. "That's how. Any woman can screw any man if she really wants to. I loved that your father didn't take advantage, but God, it also turned me on."

"You're disgusting," I said. "If you ever talk to me again . . ." Nothing more came out.

"It was the only time I've ever been in love," Mom said. "I still love him."

"Still?"

"Still."

"I know where he lives," I said. "I saw it in my head."

"He lives somewhere in Idaho, I think."

"Idaho."

"He'd love to meet you, Erin. It's the way he is." She didn't know what to say after that, and neither did I. So we said goodbye.

School was like a nightmare the next day. I woke up late and missed my first two classes, and in fourth period home ec, Brenda Arnsparger held up a picture drawn in her notebook of a huge dick with a face impaled on it, my name beneath the face. I didn't kick her ass at lunch. I was too tired, too something. A couple of weeks earlier she'd flashed me a dirty look from the pizza line, so I hit her in the face with a plate of stir fry. She was a nobody, a hopeless, bug-eyed loner who had no right to look at me like that. After our fight, she made friends with Avis and Mavis Davis, two white-trash sisters the size of Porta Potties who pretended to be Mexican, for what reason even God, I'm sure, is wondering. The Davises were mean. No one in the history of Kings County has ever stood up to them, not even guys. Now Brenda dressed like them, long plaid shirts buttoned at the neck and baggy chinos. She smoked and called people *ese* and *pinche* and spray-glued her bangs straight up. She looked like a peacock's ass.

In fifth period, Understanding Our World, Mr. Unzueta talked about Pangaea, this humongous landmass that long ago contained all seven of today's continents. He put diagrams on the overhead that showed how the shapes of the continents all fit together, like pieces of a puzzle. And it was true, they did — one big chunk of land surrounded by all this water. Then, over a long time, this big supercontinent broke into two pieces, Laurasia and Gondwana-land. Unzueta started to say something about continental drift but there was a fight outside and he went out to break it up. The land kept going on like that, I guess, pieces breaking off and drifting apart. When Unzueta came back, we watched a movie about geo-desic domes and I started crying. I got up and left for the nurse's office, told her I had a migraine and only a dark room would help. She called Dad to come get me.

But Shadow came instead of Dad. She was driving his Bronco, which even I wasn't allowed to drive.

"Does Dad know you're a junkie?" I asked her.

"I don't do junk," Shadow said.

"Don't even *try* the diabetic thing."

"I used to shoot a little," she said, "but I don't anymore."

"Oh my God! What a maggot! Where did my father meet you?"

"Look," Shadow said. She pulled the truck over. "Your dad and I like each other and we want to hang out. Are me and you gonna have to throw blows before we can get some peace?"

I slumped down in my seat. "Not if you keep out of my way," I said.

Shadow put the truck in gear. "Why are you such a bitch, any-way?"

"I have issues."

"Yeah?" Shadow looked puzzled. "Well . . . I have two left feet."

A strange silence followed, then Shadow cracked up laughing, and then I did.

"Willis Dodd isn't my dad," I said.

"So I hear. That was quite a moment you two had."

"It was something you said that made me see it. About your uterus being tilted. Which, by the way, grossed me *completely* out."

Laugh lines forked at the corners of her eyes. "Then you'll like this," she said. "I have to make adjustments when I have sex, because of the tilt. The normal angles don't work."

"I'm just going to turn my imagination right off."

"You're a virgin, huh?"

"That's none of your business."

"I guess not," Shadow said. "But you shouldn't take it out on everyone else."

"Just drop me off right here," I said. But Shadow drove on.

Dad was sitting at the table drinking whiskey when we got home. He looked morose and unfed. When he saw me he said, "Migraine, huh. Since when?"

"Why are you drinking in the middle of the day?" I asked.

"I guess it's still my house," he said. "I guess I can drink in it if I want to." He took his jackknife out of his pocket, opened the blade and set it on the table in front of him. He unbuttoned his sleeve and rolled it to the elbow. "Turn out the light," he said. "Leave me alone."

"You're making an ass of yourself," I said. Shadow looked at me hard.

"You're gonna try and find him, ain't you?" Dad asked. "Your biological fuckface."

I said nothing. What would be the point?

"Go on then," Dad said. He put the knife to his wrist. "Leave me alone. Both of you." I left Shadow to deal with him. What a piece of theater.

I don't have a lot of friends. I have no friends. The day I picked up the phone and found it dead I was about to call that public service number that rings you right back. People hate me. They started hating me early and I grew up as the girl people hated. So I did the only thing I could: I hated them back. Maybe this is sick, but when I figured out about my real dad, when I saw Idaho silhouetted in my head, the first thing I thought was: Would people hate me there too? There are so many people in California, it's such a big state to be hated in.

I took out the encyclopedia and lay with it on my bed. Idaho is between Ictinus and Idalium. Only a million people live there. It's almost all mountains. It has the deepest gorge in the country, nearly 8,000 feet beneath the peaks. The chief industry used to be mining, but now it's agriculture. It's a Republican state but they elect Democrats for governor. It has four electoral votes. It's just this side of the Continental Divide.

When I got home from school the next day, Dad, Shadow, and the fright wig twins were in the family room watching *Star Wars* on the biggest television screen I'd ever seen. X-wing fighters screeched into the picture from every direction. Wall-mounted speakers hissed with laser fire. Dad grinned like a schoolboy. "Greetings, Princess Erin."

"Greetings, Darth. What's all this shit?"

"It's new," Shadow said.

"Duh."

"Listen to that sound," Dad said. "And look at that." He pointed to the new VCR. "We taped *All My Children* for you."

"We figured you wouldn't want to watch it with us," Shadow said, "so we put the old TV and VCR in your room."

"You figured right," I said. But then I dropped onto the couch at Shadow's feet and watched the big screen with everyone else. The picture was crisp, the sound cutting, like razors through brain. It was amazing.

Dad shut everything off with the remote control and Shadow

said, "Girls, go outside. Grownups have to talk." The girls got up without a word and left. Scary.

Dad said, "About this other deal, um . . ."

"Dodd's going to help you find your biological father," Shadow said.

"I hope you'll still think of me as your father too," Dad said.

"There's this private investigator," Shadow said. "He's real good. Can I tell her the story?"

Dad grimaced. "I don't want to hear that again."

"Nothing happened," Shadow said. "We didn't do anything, just hung out a couple of times." Dad mumbled something and Shadow went ahead. She said she'd worked for an insurance company, in claims. She figured out how to file phony claims and have the checks sent to her friends. She got away with it only twice before she got caught. The company hired a private eye who got her on videotape — receiving the envelopes, cashing the checks, the whole enchilada. "He had videotape of me inside my own apartment," she said. "I was blown away." Shadow was fired but for some reason not prosecuted. Then, a few days later, the PI showed up at her door and asked her out. "Is that balls or what?" she said. Dad bristled at this, so she skipped forward. "I'm sure he could find your father for you," she said. "That's an easy job for them guys."

I said I'd think about it, which Dad didn't like. "Offer ain't open till doomsday." He remote-controlled *Star Wars* back into reeling, screeching Technicolor, and at hearing the movie, Shadow's girls came back in. I left them to themselves. Luke Skywalker is such a fag.

.   .   .

Over the next couple of weeks, Dad went crazy buying stuff for the house: a Stairmaster, a mountain climber, a Soloflex, and a treadmill. The screened-in patio became a home gym. Dad patted the minuscule ledge of Shadow's ass. "If there's a muscle in there," he said, "we'll find it." She rubbed the bowl of his paunch. "No problem finding this." It was sort of cute. Dad looked happy. I pretended to be disgusted by it all, but at night when everyone was asleep I snuck out and used the Stairmaster, dreaming, as I climbed and climbed, of showing up in Idaho a new person, skinny and without armor.

After working out just two times, Dad was stiff as a cyborg. His eyes filled with tears when he lowered himself onto the couch. We all laughed watching him, and he laughed too. "It hurts," he said. So he bought a spa. The salesman guaranteed that the whirlpool setting would turn Dad's muscles to jelly. About every ten minutes Dad assured us that it did. "Feels good," he said.

After my late-night workouts, I'd fold the spa cover back and slip in. Ten minutes of that heavenly churning water and I slept like an Egyptian.

One night while lying back in the spa, the water pounding beneath me, I opened my eyes to find Dad standing there, smiling proudly. He had a towel in his hand. "I didn't know you was out here," he said.

"I was just trying it out," I said. "I'm done." I started to climb out but Dad stopped me.

"No," he said. "Stay. I don't have to use it."

"It's okay," I said.

"Really," he said. "Stay there. Sit." He stood with hands on hips, fairly beaming. "Feels good, don't it?"

"Yeah," I said. "It's nice."

"See. I'm not such an idiot."

"I didn't say you were an idiot."

"Well." He shifted from foot to foot. "It seats eight people. I guess we could both use it."

"I guess."

Dad hung his towel on a hook and started to get in.

"Actually," I said, "I'm getting kind of hot. I think I'll get something to drink. You want anything?" He shook his head. "I'll bring it to you," I said.

"Don't bother."

I got out and wrapped myself quickly in a towel. "Okay," I said. "Well, good night." I went inside and watched from the glass door as Dad covered the spa and took a seat on the redwood steps beside it. For a long time he sat with his hands on his knobby knees, looking toward the house.

After that I kept my distance. I was waiting — I knew that — but for what I wasn't sure. I listened to the goings-on outside my bedroom door, the movies they all watched on the big screen and the songs Dad and Shadow drank and even danced to. Dad extended his credit for an old-fashioned Wurlitzer jukebox with bubbles and electric lights and stocked it with sad, chin-in-your-beer country songs for him and lava lamp acid-flashback stuff for Shadow, Janis Joplin and other dead junkies. For the first time ever, the house had a pulse.

The next time I used the spa, Shadow slipped out of the house stark naked and joined me. "That's not how you do it," she said, snapping the strap of my swimsuit top. She climbed into the tub and sprawled out like a spider, one leg bobbing gently in my lap. "Let it hit you everywhere," she said. She moaned then like some kind of barn animal and I scooted away from her. She lay back, eyes closed, taking in water and spitting it out. "No one likes you," she said. "You don't go out, there are never any guys around. What's wrong with you?" I turned the air bubbles on, the blower *whirr*ing loudly now. Shadow hollered above the noise. "You're not ugly."

"That makes one of us," I said, mostly to myself.

She reached past me and shut the whole thing off. The swirling water slowed. "Face it," she said, "you're socially retarded."

"What should I do?" I asked.

"My opinion? I'd pick out some guy at school, someone you like a little but not a lot, and make it your job to fuck his brains out. You're the terminator: Don't stop until he's totally in love with you. And trust me — at that age he will be. Then ditch him. Word will get out, and you'll have more friends and dates than you'll know what to do with."

"Are you, like, some fuck monster or something?"

"No," Shadow said. "But yours is an extreme case. I'd lay someone. Only don't fall in love. Then your ass is his, he owns you. A virgin in love? I wouldn't wish that on anyone."

"There's no one here I could fall in love with anyway," I said. "People are scummy here."

Shadow got out of the tub and stood rubbing herself with the towel until she shone pink in the moonlight. "No they're not."

Ricky Machado wasn't a complete jerk. He was in my home ec class. He whisked egg whites into soft peaks with some style, flexing his jaw because he knew it looked cool. Until he got hit by a car while he was riding his skateboard, he was medium popular.

Then he got a thigh-high cast on his leg and suddenly everyone liked him. The cast was marked with cartoons and colorful signatures like you'd expect. By Shadow's reasoning, he'd be a good choice; I couldn't *really* fall for someone who greeted people with the Vulcan peace sign.

We were supposed to be making V-neck shirts in class, but I think Ricky was making a kite. I stopped at his table and he looked up at me with pins in his mouth, eyes wide like he'd been busted. His material was skulls and crossbones on a black field. I asked if I could sign his cast.

He looked puzzled. "What are you going to write?"

"I don't know. My phone number maybe." I remembered then that I no longer had a phone, but I kept my wits. "I'll think of something."

"Yeah," he smiled. "Okay." From his backpack he took a pouch of felt-tip pens. "Pick a color," he said. I took red. Ricky scooted his leg out from under the table and I kneeled down. The only white space left was on the inside of his thigh, so I had to scooch down some. As I steadied the cast with my free hand, Brenda Arnsparger shouted, "Look out, it's a blowjob!" Ricky grabbed the back of my head and pulled me toward him. I broke loose and fell backward into the aisle. The bell rang for lunch then, and people poured by me.

Dad and Shadow drove up to Fresno the following day to see Shadow's private eye. The house was dark when they got back, the only light coming from the big screen. The girls were sprawled on the floor as usual, and I was lying like a corpse on the new couch. Shadow ignored me and dropped to the floor with her girls, who intertwined their arms and legs with Shadow's until they looked like a giant bird's nest. It was nice how they all fit to each other, how the girls went right to Shadow without a thought, how she accepted them and let them be as they would, all of a body. For his part, Dad went to his room without a word. Through the noise of the TV, I heard his door click shut at the far end of the dark hall.

The next few days creaked by. I didn't take a step toward school, and Dad said not a word. He started working double shifts, whether to keep away from me or to pay for his spending spree I didn't know. Shadow and the girls had the run of the house, blasting the TV and the jukebox, using the spa like a splash pool. I stayed in my room.

Idaho was granted statehood in 1890, the forty-third state. Its nickname was the Gem State, its bird the mountain bluebird, its flower the syringa, whatever that is. Its tree, I learned, was the Western white pine. The state song: "Here We Have Idaho."

The Nez Perce was the big Indian tribe in Idaho. They were renowned for large herds of appaloosa horses. Their leader was Chief Joseph. A cunning fighter, he defeated huge federal troops with a small band of warriors. The government kept finding stuff they wanted on Nez Perce land, though, and moved the tribe farther and farther into the desert southern regions of the state. A few young warriors rebelled by killing some settlers, and the army went after the whole tribe. Chief Joseph took all his people and fled toward Canada to escape the soldiers. They eluded the troops for nearly fifteen hundred miles, but finally they were caught, just thirty miles from the border and freedom. "I will fight no more forever," Chief Joseph said. The Nez Perce were banished to a barren, hopeless reservation, but he kept his promise.

When the letter from Shadow's PI came, Dad turned a shade of crimson as he read it. "What does it say?" I asked. Dad said nothing, so I grabbed it away from him.

> Mr. Dodd,
> Your check bounced. I hate working for the general public. Anyway, I have all the stuff you want but you're going to have to bring a cashier's check to my office to get it. It was an easy job and, as you can see by the enclosed invoice, didn't cost much. Which makes all this a pain in the ass. Why don't you get a phone?

"Do you have the money?" I asked.

Dad shook his head. "I get paid next week," he said.

"Idaho has a population of one million," I said. "It's called the Gem State. The state bird is the turkey buzzard."

"I could take a cash advance on my credit card," Dad said.

"They test nuclear weapons on the Indians there. And diseases too. Bubonic plague, black death. And they hunt them for sport. But the Indians keep smiling. They're a proud people."

"I'm sorry I've been such a terrible father."

"You haven't been terrible," I said. "I just hate my life."

"Okay," Dad said, his eyes glassy now with tears. "I'll go."

I went to my room. A few minutes later, Shadow knocked, then came in. "You should go with him," she said. "You really should."

"Will you come too?" I asked her.

She climbed onto the bed and gathered my hair at the back,

took a scrunchie from her pocket and doubled it over and over until I had the taut ponytail of a little girl. "You should probably go just the two of you," she said. "Don't you think?"

"Yeah." Then I said, "He really is a good man."

"He's a prince," Shadow said. She laughed dryly, her smile hanging a beat too long in her cheeks.

"Do you love him?" I asked.

"Sister," she said, "he knows all my angles."

It turned out that Dad didn't know Shadow's angles at all, though. When we got home from Fresno, me gripping the bright white envelope of my real father's life, the house had been cleaned out and Shadow and the girls were gone. Dad and I walked silently from room to room, pausing at the dents like fresh scars in the carpet. Everything was gone. Everything. All the rooms were empty except for clothes strewn here and there. How big our little house looked.

I sat on the family room floor where the big screen had been and cried. Dad walked the rooms again, looking, I knew, for a note. When he didn't find it, he sat back against the wall beside me. "I guess that's that," he said.

"We should call the police."

He nodded, cupped his hands to his mouth. "Police!" he called. "Hey you dumb sonsabitches!" He sat quiet for a while, his fingers absently tracing furniture outlines in the carpet. "I'm just not meant to hold on to things," he said.

"I'm going to miss her," I said.

Dad laughed. "One crazy bitch after the other. I guess that's my lot in life."

"Does that include me?" I asked.

Dad pressed the keys to the Bronco into my hand and squeezed it shut. His last possession. "It does today," he said. "About tomorrow I couldn't even guess."

I drove to the Beacon station and dropped a handful of change into the phone, punched the numbers to my father's house in Sand Point, Idaho, the area code exotic to the touch. Immediately it was answered.

Have you ever heard yourself on tape, the voice that is but isn't you? This was the voice I heard. It was almost me, but not quite. The girl laughed into the phone. "Hello?" Band music shimmied in the background, party chatter reaching me as a happy din.

"Hello," I said. "I'm calling for —"

"Hello?"

"Hello. I'm calling —"

"Daddy," the girl shouted above the noise. "The phone's doing it again." Something made of glass broke in the distance. A peal of laughter echoed. "Are you there?" the girl asked. "If you are, I can't hear you."

"I think I might be your sister," I said.

"Whoever this is, I guess you'll have to come over now. Don't worry, we'll be going late."

"Maybe someday we'll meet."

"Don't bring anything, we have plenty."

"I have to go now," I said. "Goodbye."

"Sorry, I can't hear you. If this is Tim, where are you?" She hung up.

I dropped my last quarter into the phone and tapped out my number. It too was strange, nearly forgotten. Then the recording came on. *You've reached a number that has been disconnected.* For better or worse, I knew this time I was calling home.

between angels

ABE'S SALES MANAGER at the car lot understood the importance of keeping the goal in sight, and he drilled this into the heads of all the salesmen. Months ago, he asked Abe what he wanted in life, and when Abe shrugged, his manager told him to come up with something, a Rolex or a car, something to work toward. "Put a picture of it on your mirror and look at it every morning beside your face," he said. "Let the two become one in your mind, indivisible: Abe / Audi 5000 with leather, Audi 5000 with leather / Abe. When you make your pitches, think of that car, of yourself behind the wheel, the woman at your side, the road wide open in front of you, and just see if you're not asking for the close every time you open your mouth."

"Audis don't hold their value as well as some," Abe had said.

"Think of something else, then," he said. "And show me a picture of it tomorrow morning or you're fired." Abe could think of nothing, so he went with the Rolex. He got a brochure from the jewelry store and brought it in to show his manager and then put it on his mirror as he was told. Then he promptly forgot it.

Now, packing his few undershirts and boxer shorts from the dresser, gathering toiletries, wondering which food items if any would be worth keeping with him in his car, Abe wishes he'd been more practical. But would a "Pay Rent or Quit" notice have inspired more sales success than a gold watch?

No matter. In his deeper heart, Abe credits himself for being above such obeisance to luxury. Even self-sufficiency is a bore.

Taking a last look around his apartment, Abe finds little he cares to hold on to, few things he's owned more than the two or so years he's lived here, his longest tenure at an address since the tucked away and finally forgotten days of his childhood. No family photographs hang on the walls, no memorabilia clutter the shelves. Abe indulges in a moment's self-pity considering this, just a moment's, then puts the thought away.

And almost immediately these last minutes exist to Abe only as a hole in time. What did he come into this room for? Oh yeah, a last look. Ah, to hell with that. He unfolds his eviction letter and empties into it one nostril and then the other. *Happily, I quit thee.*

On his way out of the building, Abe stops to cram the besnotted paper into the manager's mailbox. When he has it halfway through the slot, a door in the dark hallway opens. A gray-haired woman with a pillbox hat and cane stands watching him, unsure after seeing Abe's tall, careless appearance if she wants to come out any farther.

"Howdy," Abe says. "I was just leaving something. For the manager." He sets his suitcase down, picks it up. "I live here."

The woman says nothing. She waits.

"We're friends, actually," Abe says. "He asked me to leave this."

The woman seems to feel, and for a moment to share, Abe's awkwardness; not at being caught tinkering with government-protected property, but in an act that suggests an anger Abe doesn't really have. It's just another day, after all. You can laugh or . . . or what?

"Sorry," Abe says. He crumples the notice and slips it into his pants pocket. "I was just kidding around." He picks up the suitcase and leaves through the glass front door.

It occurs to Abe that he can go in any direction he likes. It occurs to him further that one direction is more or less the same as the other unless you're going a long way, all the way, even. Abe has never gone all the way. Instead, he goes a little way all the time, like everyone else. Going all the way is for the movies. Abe has a theory about people who say they're going all the way: They really only go until they're out of sight, then they die.

As Abe crosses the street in front of the building, a red sedan squeaks to a halt in front of him. The passenger-side window buzzes slowly down, revealing a man's face one line at a time, like a video image: a pad of stiff, dark curls, a heavy, wrinkled brow, eyes gleaming like obsidian chips, wide nostrils pressed nearly flat to the thick lips that smile up from a shallow jaw.

A little at a time, Abe thinks. *That could kill you too.*

"The little missus put you out?" the man asks, nodding at Abe's suitcase.

"Nope," Abe says. "I'm homeless." He starts up the walk.

The man calls after him. "I knew you weren't married," he says. "The question was a little disingenuous, forgive me."

"No problem." Abe walks on but the car surges forward and stops beside him.

"Abe, I know you're being ironic with this homeless stuff, and I like that; you take it on the chin and keep smiling. But this is a time to shut up and listen."

"How do you know my name?" Abe asks. "I don't know you."

"C'mon, get in the car," the man says. "Let's talk."

"What?" Abe scans the street, empty but for parked cars. He laughs. "I'm not getting in that car."

"I wish you would."

"Well I'm not."

"Okay," the man says. "I tried."

The rear door of the car opens and a small, crooked man gets out. Not a dwarf, just short, slight, unfinished. He holds up his hand as Abe tries to pass. Licks of brown, baby-fine hair peek out from beneath his child-size fedora. Abe pushes his hand away and sidesteps him, but the little man grabs Abe from behind by the waist of his pants and pulls him backward, slings him by his shirt-front into the car's back seat. It happens so fast, all of a single movement — yank, sling, smack, his head hard against the far door. "Hey!" The man gets calmly in beside Abe; the driver, a third man whose face Abe can't see, puts the car in gear and they're moving.

Abe looks behind: no one. Witnesses, passersby pointing from the sidewalk? None. Nobody shouting for help, no pillboxed, cane-toting old woman aghast through the glass door. No police. His suitcase lies flat and solitary in the street.

"We're not going to hurt you, Abe," the man in front says, "so there's no reason to be afraid. I just need your help with something. It's important, and you're the only one I trust it to."

"I don't know what you're talking about," Abe says. "I think I'd like to get out now."

"Relax," the man says. "Breathe or something."

Abe breathes slowly, in then out. Really, he's not that scared; weird things happen. You can fight them, but that takes a lot of energy and people tend to stare, or you can pretend they're not there, if you have a mortgage and a dog to feed. If you're beyond all that, though, beyond happiness and the expectation of it, the bumps go by pretty smoothly. In fact the bumps can be the only reminder you're taking a ride that one day will end.

"Abe, this is gonna sound funny, but I need one of God's chosen people for this job. I have reason to believe you fit that bill."

Abe has been spoken to of God before in the street. Usually people who speak of God in the street don't kidnap you.

"You don't make snuff films, do you?" Abe asks.

"Abe, you're safer here than anywhere else in the world. Lou'll see to that. Right, Lou?"

The crooked man beside Abe stares disinterestedly out the window. "No."

Abe wonders if his door has been welded shut. The bulge in Lou's coat, the gun Abe glimpsed as he was slung into the car, makes him fairly certain that it is.

"Don't listen to Lou," the man in front says. "He's just pouting 'cause I been ribbing him about that slug trail under his nose. I mean please, *that* mustache on *that* face? Lou, after we shave Abe, we'll do you, okay?"

"Shave me?"

"Don't worry about it," the man says. "That's the smallest part. There's good stuff, too. Lou, tell Abe what we got for him after he helps us out."

"A bullet in the head," Lou says.

"A bullet in the head." The man in front laughs. "Stop it, you're scaring him."

Abe has heard about snuff films from TV. They abduct people in the street, hookers and kids, your better-looking homeless, and take them out to shacks in the desert and torture them and rape them and kill them on film so people can have sex while they watch. Abe figures these films must sell for a lot of money because of the risk involved, which means it must be stuff rich people are into, which sounds about right from what he knows of the rich, which is very little.

"What is it exactly you want?" Abe asks. "I won't do porno or anything."

The man laughs. "What I want is a new start for myself and for humankind," he says. "What do you want?"

Is Abe supposed to answer this? The man waits. Lou turns to Abe, interested now.

See? Weird things. Abe could think of nothing he wanted all those months ago when his sales manager had asked him, and now again someone wants to know. Though it seems that now, facing death, his wants should be innumerable, immediate. What *does* he want? His mind races, skittering across the uncluttered surface of his life, alighting only on random faces and meaningless moments. No one person's voice calls to him, no desires rage upward.

"My throat's a little dry," Abe says. "I could go for a Pepsi."

"A Pepsi," the man says. "Smart-ass. Lou, give Abe the envelope."

Lou produces a bulging canary envelope and holds it out to Abe without taking his eyes from the scene outside the window, the squat strip mall buildings and the hurried LA traffic. "We should just do it my way," Lou says.

"Abe, take the envelope." Abe takes it, hefts the thick, paper weight of it in his hand. "Those are thousand-dollar bills in there, fifty of them. In the trunk I have nineteen envelopes exactly like that one in a nice suitcase. A Samsonite, ain't it, Lou?"

"I don't know."

"Anyway, it's nice. And it's yours, Abe. Though by the end of the day, I think you'll have forgotten about it. That's what kind of day this is going to be."

Abe labors through the calculations. There's nothing he can do that's worth a million dollars. "You sure you don't do snuff films?" he asks.

"We might in your case," says Lou.

The man in front almost leaps into the back seat. "Lou, shut the fuck up, I'm serious. Abe, don't listen to this asshole." He reaches back and slaps Lou's face, pinches his cheek hard. Lou slaps the hand away and takes up his vigil at the window. "He depends on me," the man explains, smiling now. "I found him in a trash can when he was a baby. A crooked little fuck stain lying there in banana peels and coffee grounds, grinning like a bastard. I've realized since then that I was meant to find him, he was sent to me. Like what's his name, Pinocchio, the wooden puppet that guy found and raised like a son though he wasn't even human. That's us, ain't it, Lou? Except Lou doesn't have a big nose, he's just ugly. But we've been together a long time, and he does whatever I tell him without hesitation. Which is why you should listen closely to everything I say. *Closely.* Right, Lou?"

"Yeah, yeah."

"His name's Geppetto," Abe says. He hates it when people re-member movies wrong. "And he made Pinocchio, he didn't find him."

"You watch movies?" the man asks.

"I like movies," Abe says. "The kind where no one's killed in the filming."

"So do I," the man says. "So do I. In fact I know of one you might like. But we'll talk about that later, first things first. I am Mookie. Lou you've met. Lou's sorry for throwing you in the car like he did, ain't you, Lou?"

"No."

"He's sorry," Mookie says. "And about the money, throw it out the window if you don't believe I'm giving it to you. I have more than I need. Think of it as part of your inheritance."

Abe has read about people who come into money from distant relations unknown to them. But before this fancy can get off the ground, Abe's mind flashes on the three or four bits of memory that have stayed with him — his father's slacks, the pant legs meticulously creased; heavy-bottomed highball glasses clicking with ice; a naked woman ducking behind the icebox door, laughing. But that's all, no faces. His mind won't go there. So much of him has gone into the forgetting.

"Abe," Mookie says, "I'm wondering how much you know about your heritage. Not much, I'm thinking, but I could be wrong."

"My heritage?"

"Yeah. You know, family history, genealogy, that kind of crap."

When Abe was still with him, his father didn't talk much about the past, didn't believe in it, he said. He told women he was half Greek and they seemed to like that.

"I think I'm Greek," Abe says. "About a quarter."

Mookie shakes this away. "You're a Jew," he says. "Not quarter, not half. All."

"What?" Abe hesitates at this. "How do you know? Who are you?"

"This is going to be a long day if you keep asking questions, Abe. Just trust me, I know."

"Jewish?" Abe says the word aloud again as if tasting it. Jewish. In truth, it's something he's always suspected but never pursued. Why, when he sees movies in which Nazi children are being taught to recognize Jews by skull shape and facial features, does he transpose his own face, his own skull, over the one being examined? Of course he never takes this seriously because there's always a Jew among them — that's the movie — but also he does take it seriously. In the face of the frightened Jewish boy whose identity is secret, Abe always sees himself, his own little boy's face. He knows and understands the look. He sees it also when he walks in the streets after work, in the haggard, dispossessed faces that find his and don't look away when he does but follow him until he's far out of sight, and then farther still, when he's asleep, then awake again, razor in hand at the mirror.

So Jewish. Fine. Better than fine, in fact. Who in LA doesn't want to be Jewish? But there's something else. Abe wants to ask Mookie but the words won't come. "I don't think I am."

"You're not circumcised," Mookie says. "Means nothing. Your father didn't give a shit, which you know."

The intimacy of Mookie's knowledge hits Abe only now. "Did you know my father?"

Mookie says nothing.

"How did you know him?"

Again, silence.

"Did you know me?"

"Abe, try to stay focused. We've got a lot to go over."

"If you knew us then you know we were poor," Abe says. "He had no choice."

"Hey," Mookie says. "Don't try to sell me."

"My mother left us," Abe says. "Did you know her too?"

"Your mother? Lou, wake up and shoot this guy. You win, I lose. He's too stupid to be alive."

Lou stirs from his bleary-eyed gaze at the glass. "I'll shoot him."

"Kid," Mookie continues, "that was not your mother who left you. I'm sorry to tell you this, I thought you knew, but your mother died having you. She was a good lady, religious. She wouldn't have left you."

"But she did. I was there, I should know."

"That's right, you should. But your head is so far up your ass you could lick a part in your hair. That was *not* your mother who left. That was nobody, some piece your father hooked up with. *Not* your mother. You hear me?"

"Yeah," Abe says. "I hear."

"Good. Now shake it off, I got more to tell you."

"I'm okay," Abe says. And he is. He was young when she left. Four? Maybe five? He never felt her absence like his father did, or like he felt his father's later on.

"You know him," Abe says. "Don't you?"

"Abe, shut up. Listen."

In the space of the next hour, through the walls of the Grapevine, the mountain highway north of LA, and up Highway 99 along the spine of the San Joaquin Valley, Mookie tells Abe about his grandparents, how they moved to America from a Turkish ghetto, set up house in New York City, in Queens. "They persevered," he says. "They lived. And they kept the faith, because they knew who they were." Here he starts to tell about Abe's father, but Abe interrupts.

"Don't tell me if he's dead or alive."

Mookie shrinks from this. "No? Hm. We'll see about that." He tells of Abe's father and mother marrying, her death at Abe's birth, his father bringing baby Abe to California. "Remember," he says, "your dad was a kid when he came over, so he basically grew up American. He wants to fuck, he wants to be Jimmy Cagney, he wants no part of that old-time Jew crap. So he comes to California and changes his name, and yours too. Avimelech Cohen is who you really are. Your pop thought Abe Crane would be better for show business."

"Say it again, please."

"Ah-vee-me-lech."

"Avimelech," Abe says, the syllables exotic on his tongue.

"And what do you get out of all this, Avimelech?"

Abe's momentum into the past will carry him only so far. He says nothing, gets his brain going forward again. Snuff films, he thinks. A million dollars. Inheritance.

"People give babies up all the time," Mookie says. "I make no judgments. But how old were you? Nine? Ten?"

Jewish, Abe thinks. Greek. Snuff films.

"You were ten, weren't you, Abe?" Mookie's gaze melts into the middle distance at the thought. "Jesus, what a piece of shit. Your old man earned a living, nobody was starving. I ask you this as a friend, Abe: How did that feel?"

How can Abe answer? One night when he was a boy there were some people over at the apartment drinking and having fun. One woman went on about how adorable Abe was, what a little gentleman and all that. "Fifty bucks and he's yours," Abe's father said. They bounced the joke around for a while. "How about forty bucks and a kiss?" "How about twenty bucks and five minutes in the closet?" Abe ran and hid under the kitchen sink, sobbing as quietly as he could because if they found him he would be sold or traded. Death was all he could think of. Blackness. His body ached from crying only to himself. Sometimes, when Abe is chilled, he can recall that pain in the cavity of his chest, the exact feeling.

"I don't want to talk about my father anymore," Abe says.

Mookie scratches his chin. "You don't like my 'head over here, ass over there' proposition?"

"I'm just used to the fit," Abe says. "I'll pull it out a little at a time if it's okay."

"Actually, Abe, it's not. Your father represents to you a hope that is not justified, so it's time to flush the bullshit fantasies. He didn't make it."

Didn't make it. Of course he didn't. If Abe had allowed himself to think about it, he'd have known. His father's hopes were too high, and he was imprecise, eager. He was fragile.

Didn't make it.

"I'm sorry," Mookie says. "But you had to know."

Abe looks away from Mookie, his throat knotted with feelings he'd long ago given up. "I didn't have to know," he says.

Mookie sighs. "It's that kind of thinking that got you where you are now," he says. "And if you don't mind my saying, that was your father's problem, living with illusions."

Abe watches out the window, the migrant farm workers bent between rows of grapes, holding between their legs brown paper bundles of fruit that will become raisins. Into the sun-bright horizon they work, on and on, and then they die.

"There's nothing wrong with illusions," Abe says. "Sometimes they sustain us."

"I know," Mookie says, "but they're not supposed to. That's what's wrong with them. And with us."

They drive for a while in silence. Abe is exhausted, depleted of whatever buoyant goo keeps the body afloat in the world. He feels like he's going down, down, a fifty-foot Mickey Mouse shot through and losing air over Macy's, flatulent, falling, frowning into the crowd as his empty balloon body pours onto their parade.

Just outside Bakersfield, Mookie spills it, the five Ws and the *H* of what it's all about. "You're a descendant of Moses," he says to Abe. "From the tribe of Levi, specifically. That's why I need you."

"But I'm not religious," Abe says.

Mookie waves this away. "According to the Bible," he says, "the Levites are the inheritors of God. You belong to Him. And one day, He to you. If you buy that line."

"What does that mean?" Abe asks. "He to me?"

Mookie grins. "Good things." The Levites served as priests and kept the temple, he explains. Kept the faith, so to speak. They were the handlers of the Ark of the Covenant, which contains the stone tablets inscribed by God with the ten commandments. "The ark is supposed to be the living vessel of God on Earth," Mookie says. "Which sounds important, no?"

Abe agrees that it does.

Only the Levites, Mookie says, can touch the Ark, or even look upon it uncovered. "Some guy named Uzzah grabbed it to keep it from falling when the Hebes were carrying it," he says, "and God fucked him good. A lightning bolt right up the ass." The chosen, Mookie says. Keepers of the faith. He repeats these phrases often, wants Abe to hear them, drink them in.

"Do you believe all that?" Abe finally asks.

"Let's put it this way," Mookie says, "I'm too smart to buy it wholesale, but I'm too smart to ignore it too. Especially now that I have the Ark."

"What do you mean, you have the Ark?"

"I have the Ark."

"The Ark you were just talking about?"

"You bet your ass."

"Of the Covenant?"

"Fucking yes, I said."

The Ark of the Covenant, Abe thinks. The ten commandments. Jewish and Moses and God. And him, Abe Crane Jr. Or rather, Avimelech.

"You want me to open it, don't you?" Abe says.

"I'd like you to."

Abe suddenly remembers a movie, ghosts tear-assing out of the Ark and melting Nazis, a smorgasbord of death.

"What if it isn't supposed to be opened?" he asks.

"That movie's full of shit," Mookie snaps. "Don't be a chump."

Abe looks away. "What movie?"

"You know what movie! Don't insult me." Mookie sits back in his seat. "Have faith. That's important."

Faith. Abe's supposed to have faith. An hour ago he was a newly homeless, possibly Greek ex–car salesman, and now he's supposed to open the Ark of the Covenant. How is faith possible in such a world?

But weird things happen. Probably weirder than this, even. So Abe goes along.

"I'll open it," he says. "I don't care."

"Well thank you," Mookie says, "but there's more to it than that. From everything I've read, seen, and heard, you're supposed to approach the Ark with absolute confidence in your right to do so. You are its rightful heir. Understand?"

Abe shakes his head. "Not really, but I'll open it. I had nothing planned for today."

"I don't think you're taking this seriously, Abe, so I'll say it again, I want to be clear." Mookie speaks slowly. "*I* have the Ark. *You* are going to open it. If the story of the Ark is true — and the fact that I have it in my possession is very suggestive, I think — then your belief in both God and yourself *cannot* be tainted when you touch it. If it is, you will be dead, fucked in the ass with big fucking splintery pine trees all day, every day, probably for eternity. Do you understand *that*?"

Abe nods. "Yeah," he says. "I'm beginning to."

"So do you believe me that you are who I say you are, or do I seem like someone who does not know that of which he speaks?"

Abe isn't sure if he believes Mookie or not. He wants to — the past he left behind in LA is all nonsense now — but you can't just decide to believe. So he says nothing.

"Have a little faith," Mookie says.

Abe considers this. "Faith in you?"

"In yourself," Mookie says. "And in God."

Abe laughs. "It seems like faith in you is more important."

"What's that supposed to mean?"

"It means if you're wrong about me, I'm going to get what Uzzah got. Right? If all the rules apply?"

Mookie thinks this over. "Technically that's right," he says. "But if I'm wrong about you, then maybe I'm wrong about the Ark too, and none of it'll matter. You'll walk away with your million and I'll have my answer."

"Your answer to what?"

"To the big question. Why do you think I'm doing all this?"

Abe shrugs. "I assumed it was for money."

"Money?" Mookie's face reddens. "Fuck you, you know that? Just . . . fuck you and don't talk to me." He faces front, shaking his head. His ears flush through his olive skin. "I kill people, Abe. Do you know what that means?"

"The snuff film business is picking up?"

Mookie sits silent a moment before answering. "I just want to believe in God," he says. He waits again, thinking, then speaks. "But I need proof. Ain't that a piece of shit?"

"Mook," says Lou, "let's junk this whole plan. I don't like it."

"We discussed this already," Mookie says.

"I don't like it," Lou says again. "Let's just shoot this guy and sell that fucking box."

"You know that's not gonna happen."

Lou turns again to the window, silent.

"Don't pout," Mookie says. "You know I hate that."

Lou turns to Abe. "What are you looking at?"

Through Abe's protests, Mookie gives him a summary of his father's life after leaving Abe at the county orphanage: His father opened a nightclub with two other men. He was the front, the owner as far as everyone knew — snapping his fingers for rounds on the house, monkeying around on stage as he introduced the acts. The real owners did not wish to be known.

Then Mookie says something so fantastic that the hole Abe dug long ago in his heart, a grave of sorts, nearly fills. "Your pop was in a movie," Mookie says. "It was shot in his club. He played the muggy host. The film's called *Uptown, Downtown*. You probably never heard of it."

Abe's father in the movies. It's almost a miracle. Though he was handsome, a perfect fit for the pictures, really, he seemed always to suffer the knowledge that the big prizes were beyond him. Even as a child Abe knew this. It was his father's sadness, and Abe's too.

"I guess he did the right thing," Abe says. "Leaving me."

"It wasn't right," Mookie says. "It was easy. There's a difference."

"He took me to the pictures every week," Abe says, remembering only now that his father always said "picture," never "movie." "He liked to look at the clothes. The way the actor held his glass, ordered dinner. Dad measured a picture's success by how much style it had. He loved the idea of cigarette girls. His club had cigarette girls, I bet."

"Immortality," Mookie says. "That's what he wanted. It's a drive satisfied by most through children, but your dad had the unfortunately common desire to do this through film. A more flammable medium, eh, Lou?"

"A waste of time if you ask me," Lou says.

"What do you mean, 'flammable'?" Abe asks.

"I mean *Uptown, Downtown* didn't make it to VHS," Mookie says, "and recently there was a tragic fire at the studio where the original print was warehoused."

Abe thinks about what all of this means. "You have it, don't you?" he asks.

Mookie doesn't answer. They drive for a while in silence, the road suddenly smooth beneath them.

Just outside Delano, Mookie thumps the driver's arm and he exits the highway, drives to a defunct gas station, a cinder block building with boarded windows. Smashed pumps stand rusting in the sun. Outside Abe's window is a door: *Men*, it reads, the letters scratched childishly into faded blue paint.

"See that Volks over there?" Lou says to Abe. He points behind the building to the carcass of an old Volkswagen sitting with empty eye sockets on naked hubs. "A thousand bucks I can piss over that car."

"What?" Mookie says. "A thousand! It ain't even got tires, for Christ's sake. Bet him that Mustang over there, Abe."

"I ain't bettin' no Mustang. I said the Vee-dub."

"I'm a millionaire now, right?" Abe asks.

"It's your money," Mookie says.

"Then why not ten thousand?" Abe says. "Or fifty?"

"I wouldn't have pegged you for a gambler," Mookie says. "But it makes a certain sense now that I know you better. I like you, Abe."

"Fifty grand," Lou snickers. "I'm gonna fuck your ass."

Mookie and Abe lean against the red sedan and watch as Lou unfurls a stream of urine that arcs cleanly over the top of the Volkswagen, *thwap*ping the hard dirt on the other side.

Mookie shakes his head. "Tsk, tsk, tsk. Gambling is for jackasses, Abe. You think Lou'd bet if he wasn't sure he could do it? A man comes to you for a bet, he's playing you for a fool. You take the bet to him, you're hoping to play him for a fool, right? No one bets to lose. Unless there's a bigger payoff down the line, which is another story. The point is, it's a mirage. A chimera — which is something that looks real but ain't, which you know all about. I got no sympathy."

Lou zips up proudly, giggling. Mookie says, "You laugh, Lou. You know why Lou's laughing, Abe? He knows I'm not completely right. Anything is possible when someone stands to gain. Right, Lou?"

"I coulda taken the 'stang," Lou says. Then to Abe he says, "Fifty G's, big shot. Cash'll do."

"You'll take a rain check," Mookie says. He pops the trunk and takes from it a paper bag, steers Abe into the bathroom with a friendly hand. Inside, he shakes from the sack a pair of scissors, soap, a can of shaving cream, a bag of disposable razors, pajamas wrapped in plastic, and a pair of new white sneakers. He puts the pajamas and sneakers back in the sack and rolls it up. "We're gonna cut your hair off, then shave you from head to toe, every inch. Okay?"

"You didn't say anything about every inch," Abe says.

"*Caveat emptor*, Abe. That's what the big book says to do, and that's the script we're following today. If this thing doesn't work out, it ain't gonna be from not following directions."

Lou hacks roughly through Abe's hair, stretching each fistful taut then closing the scissors slowly so that every strand feels yanked by the root. "Cut faster," Abe says, and Lou does. Soon Abe's back is sore from bending down for the shorter man.

"My father and I used to go every week for a haircut," Abe says. "I forgot about that. Yeah, Saturday mornings. No matter what the night before was like, Dad always rousted me and pushed me down the street to the barber shop the next morning." Abe laughs. "That's pretty cool, huh? I forgot about that."

"That's all I can do with these," Lou says. He pushes Abe's head away, drops the scissors in the sink.

"Okay," Mookie says. "We gotta shave you now. Down on your knees, you tall sonofabitch."

Abe slogs his foot against the floor. "There's piss everywhere."

Mookie swipes his own shoe through it. "Yeah. Fucking gas stations. Ain't even in business anymore. Okay, come here." He kicks the toilet lid down and stands on it, sprays Abe's head with shaving cream and takes a razor in his giant hand and steadies Abe by the jaw. Mookie's touch with the razor is surprisingly light; it skates smoothly across Abe's scalp. Dollops of cream speckled with dark hair plop to the floor.

"You're pretty good at that," Abe says.

"You have a nice scalp," Mookie says. "Clean. No scars." Abe feels his head. Except for a few bumps in the back, it is smooth. "It spirals at the top," Mookie says, "like your head's trying to flush itself down a toilet only there ain't no hole. Lou, come here and check out Abe's head."

Abe bends down so Lou can see. Lou palms his head by the crown and rubs side to side, like juicing an orange. "Not bad," he says.

"What do you mean 'not bad'?" Mookie says. "It's perfect."

"It's a little lumpy in back," Lou says.

Mookie pulls Abe upright and inspects him again. "That's the way heads are. It's ideal. Let's shave *you* and count the lumps. Like a fucking cauliflower, I bet. Cakes of dandruff, blistery, boily shit everywhere. Makes me sick thinking about it."

"I wasn't making comparisons," Lou says. "I just don't think it's perfect."

"Eczema," Mookie says. "Psoriasis. You misshapen fuck."

"Hagler," Lou says. "There's a perfect head."

"You've never even seen Hagler's head," Mookie says. "TV. Everything looks perfect."

Lou's eyes widen with protest. "Hagler's head? I never seen Hagler's head? Then whose head did I hold a gun to? Sugar Ray's? He had an afro."

Mookie thinks about this. "Yeah," he says. "I forgot. Still, I'll put Abe's head up there with Hagler's any day."

"How about Yul Brynner?" Abe says.

"You're such a product," Mookie says. "Get undressed."

Abe is not often without a shirt. Right off Mookie senses something's wrong. "Doff 'em, buddy. Giddyup." Lou kicks him in the ass to hurry him. Abe frees each button slowly, then lets the shirt fall to his waist, where it hangs tucked into his pants.

"Jesus," Mookie says.

"It was a long time ago," Abe says. "I don't think about it."

Mookie's finger lightly explores a scar at Abe's shoulder, almost afraid, as if the wound was fresh. There are sixty or so in all, little craters of melted skin on his back and shoulders, a sprinkling on his left side, three on his ass. They're from cigarettes mostly, but a few are from the open flame of an antique lighter that Abe himself spirited from a pawn shop and foolishly allowed to be taken away. All the scars are in back, out of sight.

"Your father?" Mookie asks.

"No. Some kids in a foster home. It's no big deal. They don't hurt."

The silence is awkward. Mookie breaks open the pack of razors and hands Abe the can of cream. "You go ahead," he says.

Abe is not a hairy man — a small patch on his chest and a dusting on his shoulders and lower back — but as he shaves himself, he understands in a new way that the body is not meant to be scraped clean of its cover. It's painful, sure, scraping on delicate skin, and the nicks, but also it's unfamiliar, discomforting, seeing his own body from so many angles, new perspectives. It's another kind of pain.

Finished, Abe dabs his wadded shirt at a dozen or so points of blood. Then Mookie says, "The toes. Fingers too." Abe shaves these, his eyebrows, and his face for the first time today. Mookie approaches his back with a fresh razor. "Be still," he says. As with

Abe's head, Mookie's stroke is sure and painless, artful, even, around his scars. "You got a pimple," he says to Abe. "I'm afraid to shave over it." Abe feels Mookie's fingers squeeze together at his back, the pinch, then the burst that ripples across his skin.

"*Ow!*"

"That's something I never done to anyone before," Mookie says.

When he's finished, Mookie takes Abe's shirt, wets it under the faucet, and wipes Abe of the shaved hair. The cold stings his back and sides, startles his shoulders, but by the time it reaches the backs of his legs down to his ankles, it is soothing and welcome. "This *does* feel sort of Biblical," Abe says.

"Hold that thought," Lou says, " 'cause you ain't done."

Mookie nods at Abe's groin. "And," he says, "you may not be thrilled by this, but we gotta do your ass."

"Where did you read this?" Abe asks. "What chapter? Surely it's not meant literally."

"It's very specific, and it says every hair."

"What about the scrotum?" Lou says. "Someone's gonna have to pluck it."

"It'd be a tough shave," Mookie agrees. Then he says, "Abe, I'm gonna let you handle the rest any way you see fit. Just make sure it's all gone. We'll wait outside. Put your clothes on and come out when you're done."

Lou snips at the air with the scissors, grinning. "He's supposed to be circumcised."

Mookie hangs his head. He waits one, now two beats too long — Abe begins to reevaluate his day — then Mookie says, "No, I can't do that to Abe."

"Be easier to keep clean," Lou says.

Mookie pushes him out the door. "Lou's just trying to be thorough," he says. "For your own protection." He starts out, but stops. "Abe, you think there's a heaven?"

Abe shrugs, and the two men stand in silence a moment, both wondering what it might be like. Is Mookie's picture different than Abe's? Beyond doubt, Abe knows that the image of Heaven for his father would have been that of a stage, an orchestra behind, a white-lit circle into which he would step, tuxedoed and pomaded, and out of which he would squint into the darkness at the faces shining up at him. Abe's own picture is the standard: clouds and angels, robes, the deep, disembodied voice of God rumbling in the distance. The chairs are gilded and too big, not at all comfortable.

Mookie thumps the driver on his shoulder with the back of his hand when they get back in the car. The driver — a Middle Easterner of some type, dun-colored skin, a mask of dark stubble — turns to him and Mookie's hands launch into a series of pointed gestures. Sign language. The driver is deaf. Before Mookie is done fingering his sentence, the man nods and looks away.

"We're stopping for Slurpees," Mookie says. He turns back to Abe. "You like Slurpees, Abe?"

"Sure," Abe says. "I'll stick it between my legs to cool my balls down."

"Did you pluck 'em?" Lou asks. Abe ignores him.

"You know what the most popular Slurpee flavor is?" Mookie asks.

Abe shrugs. "Cherry?"

"That's right, good. You know the second?"

"No."

"Coca-Cola. Third is anything blue." Mookie shakes his head at this, amused. "As a rule, Abe, blue things taste like shit."

The driver parks beside rather than in front of the store. As Mookie disappears through the swinging doors, Lou quickly unholsters his gun and swings it around into Abe's ribs, delivering three sharp blows before Abe is folded over to one side, his body rigid, breath coming not at all. When he finally snatches a quick breath, it sears his lungs and swells through his chest like hot tar.

"Want to have a drink up there?" Lou mocks in singsong. "He doesn't give a shit about you, if that's what you're thinking. And don't believe all this chosen one bullshit, either. Mook ain't for sure if you're one of these Levite faggots. There's no way for anyone to know for sure — the records don't exist — so if I was you I'd pray that Ark ain't real. Or else duck when you open it."

When Abe has his breath again, he covers his ribs, scoots close to the door, away from Lou.

"When you open that thing and there's nothing in there but a bunch of monkeyshines, the old man's gonna forget all about you. And I'm gonna shoot your ass." He smiles at this. "Mook'll be a little cheesed at first but he ain't gonna lose sleep over it. *I* know him. He's like me; we're the same. You don't know shit."

"What does he want the Ark for?" Abe asks, thinking — he can't help it — of the movie, world domination, that stuff.

A vague smile creases Lou's face. "Wait till you hear," he says. His grin widens slowly, inching outward, and soon he's bouncing from the waist in tiny, crooked bows, crazed with silent laughter, breathy and tight, a twisted figure of ugly, evil, insidious joy. "You ever hear the sound of elephants flying?" he asks. He leans in close to Abe but Abe stays back, watchful, protecting his ribs. "Wait till you fucking hear."

No one talks for a long way up the valley. The truck-rutted highway jounces Abe's eyes shut. Questions fly at him from some inner darkness, one after the other, faster than he can field them. They whiz past him like comets, stars firing past to die in the distance. He follows them, chasing, as though they were answers and not questions at all. And he runs, runs into the blazing sky, until finally he stops, suddenly in darkness again, standing, he somehow knows, at a precipice into which he'll certainly fall with one more step. He calls out his name, Abe, Abe. But hears nothing, no echo. Then he shouts, Avimelech. A voice calls back to him, not his own but his father's: *Yes.*

Needles of light pierce the blackness now, needles that become spears, spears that thicken to columns, columns that unfold into sheets, sheets that hang brilliant and shimmering on all sides of Abe, and he sees, finally, that he's not standing before a spiky gorge or a bottomless pit at all, but before a stage of some sort. As the lights go down and the music rises, a stillness grips Abe from the inside. His eyes open. They've stopped.

"Abe, wake up." Mookie's voice. "Time for your *mikvah.*"

"Yeah," Lou says. "Wake up, dummy. Let's go for a swim."

"I wasn't asleep," Abe says.

"Sure you weren't," Lou says. "You practically snored the car in half."

"That's not true," Abe says. "I was somewhere else, but not asleep."

Lou notices Mookie listening. "Okay," he says to Abe, "maybe you didn't snore, but you were fucking sleeping and don't tell me you weren't."

"I wasn't."

"Mook, I'm gonna shoot him."

"What do you care if he was sleeping or not?" Mookie says.

"I *don't* care," Lou says. "It's just he shouldn't lie to us."

"I'm not lying."

"You were having myoclonic spasms, assface. That's sleeping."

"That's almost sleeping," Mookie says.

"You're taking his side?" Lou says. "Over me?"

"I'm just correcting your use of the term."

"I was outside myself," Abe says. "But it wasn't a dream. I was here but not here."

Lou smirks. "'I was here but not here.' Well now you *are* here and you're gonna wish you wasn't. Get out of the fucking car."

Abe pulls the handle and his door opens. It wasn't even locked.

The green-water river, wide and shallow, gentles by through the overhanging trees. Voices echo in the distance, maybe a few feet away, maybe a mile. "Where are we?" Abe asks.

"The Kings River," Mookie says. "C'mon." He starts down a dirt path toward the water. Lou puts a fist in the small of Abe's back and they follow.

At the water's edge, Mookie again gives Abe the command. "Strip."

Abe removes his clothes without argument. "Now what?"

"Now this." Lou gets a leg behind Abe and pushes, and into the water goes Abe. His head hits the surface decently hard, but the water's warmth softens the fall. The sand below embraces him as he kneels in the friendly tug of the current. He stands, shakes his head to shed the water from his hair, which the breeze reminds him isn't there.

Abe staggers back onto the bank. "I bet you enjoyed that," he says to Lou.

Lou grins. "I did." He holds out the plastic-wrapped package of pajamas. Abe reaches for them, arm outstretched, and in this moment of imbalance Lou again pushes Abe backward, into the water.

Abe stands, wipes his eyes. "What the hell?"

"You've got to go under three times," Mookie says. "That's a *mikvah*. Three dunks in a natural water source." He turns to Lou now. "But you don't have to be so rough about it."

"Rough? You think that's rough?"

"You could be nicer," Mookie says.

"Nice? What the hell are you talking about? Why should I be nice? I *ain't* nice."

"I know," Mookie sighs. "You are what you are."

Abe is on the bank again.

"That's right," Lou says. "I am what I am." He whirls around and kicks Abe hard in the ass, raises his leg and kicks at him again, shoving him toward the water with his foot. "And this jerk is who he is and you are who you are, even if you forgot."

Abe notices then the three men emerging from the trees behind them, all shirtless and tanned brown as dirt, all of them carrying tallboy beer cans. The lead man, with two teeth missing, one up, one down, puffs his chest, scowling now. "What the hell's going on here?" he says. His body is rangy but dense, his hair, like his eyes, wild and bright from the sun. Abe has seen reasonable men collapse into the dark, animal parts of themselves when they think they're away from the eyes of the world. He doubts these men were ever reasonable.

"I said what the fuck is going on? What are you picking on that tall guy for?"

"River thugs," Lou says. "I hate river thugs."

The gap-toothed man smiles. "You hate what?" He looks back at his friends, excited.

"You heard me," Lou says.

"Nothing's going on," Mookie says. "We were just leaving. Abe, put those jammies on."

The lead thug steps into the ring of Abe, Mookie, and Lou as Abe slips into the pajama pants. "I want to know what the fuck is going on," the thug says. "This is private property." The men behind laugh. The man plays to them. "You guys doing some homo-type stuff with this boy? 'Cause I've been deputized to whip any trespassers and homos I find on this property."

Lou reaches into his jacket and Mookie calls out, "Lou, no!" And before Abe even sees the gun, he hears a shot *crack* loud off the water. Lou's body snaps backward, then quickly recoils forward until he's bent nearly double. He drops to one knee on the dirt, his face empty.

From the trees, a fourth man leaps out, giddy, calling to the others. "I shot him! Did you see that? I shot that fucker. He was going for a gun, you saw. And I shot his ass. Hoo-eee!"

Lou falls to his side in the dirt, his face turned away, to the water. The gap-toothed thug stands above him, unbelieving. "Darryl fucking shot him," he says.

"Don't use my name, jerkhole," says Darryl.

Mookie pushes the gap-toothed thug away from Lou. "Aw, shit," he says. He sits beside his friend in the dirt, takes him by his waist and his good shoulder and lays him back into his lap at the water's edge. "Goddamnit, Lou," he says. "It hurts, I know, but you're gonna be okay." He opens Lou's jacket. "It's just a shoulder shot. What caliber is it?" he asks the guy with the gun.

"Twenty-two," the guy says, suspicious, on guard. He stiffens his aim at Mookie. "And you just be still," he says. "Don't try anything."

"You hear that, Lou? A twenty-two." He laughs. "You believe the nerve of these river pussies shooting someone with a twenty-two?"

Lou, smaller than ever against Mookie's big chest, hardly a bundle in his arms, manages a nod. "Pussies," he says. He coughs, and Mookie wipes his eyes. "It hurts," he says.

Mookie bends over and kisses Lou's head, smoothes his hair. "I know, buddy, I know." When he sits up he is suddenly pointing Lou's gun at the guy with the twenty-two, who is still pointing at him.

"Be still," the guy says to Mookie. "I just want to split, okay?"

Mookie's eyes harden into a look of pure hatred, but also the most amazing expression of love Abe has ever seen. "Run," Mookie says.

The lead thug nods. "C'mon, Darryl," he says to the shooter. He backs into the trees, eyes locked on Mookie. Darryl does likewise. When they hit the relative darkness of the woods, the tentative shuffles of their feet are all at once noisy thumps of a dead sprint. The shooter's voice trails after. "Quit saying my name, asshole!"

"Wait up in the car," Mookie says to Abe. "Let me get Lou together, here. Throw me that pajama top."

Abe takes the shirt off, gives it to Mookie, then starts up the path to where they parked. "Wait," he says. "What about my *mikvah*? Did I go under three times?"

Mookie's pained look finds the middle distance between Abe and Lou. "I don't know," he says. He looks confused. "I can't think."

Abe goes back down the path, slips out of his pajama bottoms, the legs muddy now at the cuffs. He dives into the river, head first, arms outstretched. The water closes quickly behind him.

The warehouse stands before them in a row of maybe a dozen others just like it, tall, metal, brick-colored, with an overhanging roof. Warehouses like these are all they've seen in the two or three miles since leaving the highway. Abe has never been to Fresno, but this is about what he would have guessed.

Mookie buzzes his window down, which only lets in the heat. "A little primer," he says. "The Ark itself is just a box. It's made of wood, covered inside and out with gold. The lid is called the mercy seat. *That* should be something to see: two cherubim, solid gold, with wings that stretch across the ark from tip to tip. Two angels of solid gold. Imagine." Mookie shakes his head and Abe can almost see in his eyes the angels disappearing in a roil of snowflakes, like a child's toy. "You're gonna find one big crate in there," he says. "Inside that is another crate. I'm not sure if the staves are in there or not but it doesn't matter, they're just big sticks. Anyway, inside the second crate should be the Ark. I want you to open the two outer crates, then lift the mercy seat off the ark. There should be a bunch of other stuff in there too, table settings only fancy. And the tablets . . ." He shakes his head. "Man, I wish I was you. Check this out: They may or may not be made of solid sapphire. And listen to this: They're supposed to be carved all the way through. You know what that means?"

"No."

"What about the letters that make a circle? There are some. What happens to the middles of the circles if the tablets are cut all the way through?"

"What?"

"That's the thing. Nobody knows for sure. A lot of smart guys think they'll be right there, suspended in space. Can you fucking imagine?"

The supernatural weight of what he's about to do suddenly hits Abe. "Are you sure it's okay for me to be doing this?" he asks. "I mean, I don't even know if I believe in God. I think I do, but . . . I don't know. And you said I had to for sure or —"

"I don't have time to send you to Jew school to find your faith, Abe. I need this now." Mookie sinks into silence a moment. "I've done some things, Abe. If my life was a movie, it'd have the snuff crowd on their knees with their faces in bags." His eyes cloud here with the look Abe saw at the river, confusion, yes, and hatred, but more than that. "Actually it is a movie, Abe. And I watch it over and over because I can't block it out. I *can't* forget."

"I'm going to do it," Abe says.

"No shit," Lou says.

"Be careful," Mookie says. "If the tablets are in there, *don't* touch them. Just put the mercy seat back and replace the lid on the inside crate. You got it?"

Abe nods. "Then what?"

"Then . . ." Mookie's eyes brighten, become dumb. "We'll know." He rubs his stubbly cheek, smiles meekly. He drops a heavy hand onto Abe's bald head, strokes his forehead gently with his scratchy thumb. "Think of it, Abe: We'll *know.*"

It seems Abe should say something to Mookie, something to thank him, though the course of the day is not yet run and could still lead anywhere. Anywhere at all.

"This is better than what I was going to do today," Abe says.

"Abe," Mookie smiles. "Avimelech. This is a wonderful service you're doing for mankind. And for me."

Lou stirs beside Abe, restless. "The both of you make me sick," he says. He gets out of the car and stands with his back against the window. Mookie's way-too-big jacket hangs on him like a dress, but it covers the makeshift bandage.

"I think you know what I have for you when you're finished," Mookie says. "Besides the money."

Abe smiles, hopeful. "My father's movie?"

"I watched it a couple of times. Believe me, it's something you'll want to see."

"Does it have style?" Abe asks.

"Up the ass, kid. It should be on fucking cable every night."

Suddenly Abe is at that precipice again, looking out into the void for his father, listening for his voice, thinking about him, wondering about his life. This time he doesn't need to call out his name to feel his presence, to forgive his absence. The movie is enough.

"You ever have feelings of déjà vu?" Abe asks.

"Kid," Mookie says, "my whole life is déjà vu."

"I feel like I've already seen my father's movie," he says, "like I know it, every frame. Like all the characters are people I've known but have forgotten. Is that weird?"

"Weird," Mookie says. "Yeah. But that don't mean bad."

Abe and Mookie look at each other and it's as if Abe knows

Mookie's every thought, just as Mookie no doubt knows Abe's. "I wish he would have kept me," Abe says.

Mookie's a smart man; he recognizes a time for not saying anything, for a shared and unnamed look. Once again, Abe is grateful.

He's grateful, so he asks: "Why do you want the Ark so bad?"

Mookie turns this over a moment, then a moment longer, as if weighing his trust in Abe, his faith that the truth will do no harm. "Satan wasn't always evil," he says. "Did you know that?"

Abe shakes his head. It sounds familiar.

"It's true. Before man came along, Satan was an angel in God's service like any other angel. But God, I don't know, He got bored or something, something was missing for Him, so He created man and put him above the angels on the food chain, so to speak. He told the angels, 'You guys go live among man now and serve him.' But Satan didn't want to go. He said, 'God, I want to stay by your side. I don't want to leave you to serve man. Who the fuck is he, I should serve him?' But God don't like to be argued with — these were the days before mercy — so He cast Satan out of Heaven altogether, into Hell. And so pained is Satan at being separated from the God he loves, he resigns to fuck with God's creation for eternity. You see what I'm saying, Abe? Love gives rise to evil too, not just good. We don't mean for it to happen, it just does."

Abe nods, not fully understanding the meaning of Mookie's story but feeling the rightness of it.

"A lot of incidental things come out of love," Mookie says. "Indifference is one."

Before Abe can think to stop himself, he runs through the index of faces he's known — of course he hasn't really forgotten them — looking for Mookie, as he is now, as he might have appeared back then. But he can make no connection.

"How did you know my father?" Abe asks.

Mookie lowers his head in thought, then looks Abe in the eye. "I didn't," he says.

Abe doesn't understand, must have misheard. "Then how do you know so much about me?" he asks. "About my father? Everything?"

"I know things, Abe. That's what I do. It's who I am."

"What? What kind of bullshit is that?"

Lou puts his face to the glass, crooked grin in place, dark, evil eyes smiling. *You see?*

Questions flood through Abe once again — he can no more hold them back than part the Red Sea — but the energy to ask them, to rethink things, is beyond him now. And whatever answers he gets will come too late. He wonders if any answers exist at all, if they have ever existed. He feels as if he's been cut loose from the earth just as he was starting to really feel it beneath his feet.

"You want to save the world?" Abe asks.

"Some people think Jesus already did it," Mookie says. "But I think it needs doing again. Don't you?"

Abe thinks about this — maybe it does, maybe it doesn't — and an answer seems near, but before it takes shape within him, Mookie is out of the car, beckoning, calling Abe to the job he may or may not have been born to do.

A claw hammer, mallet, and pry bar lie beside the crate on the cement floor. Abe takes up the pry bar. This is definitely going all the way, he thinks. Then he stops. Already something is wrong. "The crate has screws," he calls out.

Muffled curses outside the door. "Hold on," Mookie hollers.

The car trunk *pups* open, then *chicks* hollowly shut. More cursing. Then Mookie's voice. "Phillips or straight-slot?"

"Phillips."

Mookie comes in scowling, as if the screws were Abe's doing. He pushes a cordless drill at Abe and walks wordlessly away.

Abe removes only twelve screws and the walls of the outer crate drop neatly away. Can the Ark itself be as well designed? He unseats the lid of the inside crate easily with the pry bar. The nails are old, with square heads and shafts, like small railroad spikes. He removes the top.

Wrappings of blue and purple and red cloth drape loosely over what appears to be a great chest. The fabric peaks sharply in the middle, then falls on either side until stretching at last to mound over the towering figures at the ends. The coarse, fraying linen is stiff and sharp to the touch, spun through with fine bands of gold.

Abe undrapes the fabric, somehow not breathless or trembling or at all fearful because it can't be true, this river of bullshit and pain can't have led to where Abe stands now, before what must surely be the true Ark of the Covenant. At either end, angels bow with outstretched wings that sweep toward each other, their feathers staggered like a bird's, flipped upward at the tips. In Abe's imaginings, the Ark was more severe, inelegant, less intricate in detail. The angels of this ark could as easily have been plucked from the air and dipped in a syrup of fine gold as forged and carved by ancient tools.

God, Abe thinks. Moses and my father and God.

Wedging the pry bar beneath one end of the mercy seat, Abe heaves on it, wrestles it to the side. The ark coughs a cool, dusty breath. Then everything is still. Inside and out, all across creation maybe, not a sound, not a rustle of leaves or scuff of a shoe. Silence, empty and pure.

The tablets lay stacked, the top one askew from the bottom. Lord, the size of them! Like headstones. Funereal slabs of deep blue rock, roughcast at the sides with chipped edges. The surface is smooth but undulate, gently swelling and dipping like a quiet sea. Moses was to have carried these? What size a man he must have been! When Abe thinks of his father, his grandfather, the line of men that begins with him and goes backward, he sees them getting smaller as they recede into the past. Isn't that what objects do with distance? Abe knows that man grew larger over time, but the opposite feels true to him now. The man who carried these tablets down that mountainside, who saw God and understood what that meant, is little relation to him.

Despite Mookie's warning, Abe reaches into the Ark and touches the words. He does this by impulse, by instinct, more easily than he touches or even looks at his own body. As though the tablets are truly his.

The characters, Hebrew he supposes, cleft deeply into the slab's face, the edges blackened as though by fire. From a right margin that slopes aggressively inward, the letters march to the left, arms raised, hands hanging limply as if being led. Never, to Abe's knowledge, has he seen a Hebrew word. (The subtitles on the Manischewitz labels at the grocery, is that Hebrew?) And of the ten commandments, maybe he could name seven. But as he feels with his own fingers the words of God, touches the undeniably empty space that holds fast the islands of blue stone in the circular letters, the meaning of each line is as clear to Abe as if it had come first from his own tongue.

Don't kill.

And don't cheat.

And don't steal.

And don't lie.

And don't lust for what you cannot have.

"Abe!" Again, Mookie's voice, this time a vibration through the metal wall. "Abe!"

Abe makes no answer. He replaces the mercy seat and covers it with the fraying cloth, then the crate's lid. Lou's small body bends into the light of the open door. "He looks okay," he says.

Mookie steps from behind Lou and into the room. "Abe? Are they in there?"

Lou follows Mookie in, and as if Abe were seeing himself in the mirror, he understands the fear in the tiny man's face, the terror and the longing, already the longing, for what he's about to lose.

"Abe," Mookie says. "Are they in there?"

Abe says nothing. He is voiceless, without gesture or language enough to answer.

"Abe?"

Mookie. Abe reaches out to his friend, to touch him as he has been touched, if only he could.

But Mookie stops. "They're there," he says, his eyes soft now, glowing like distant stars.

Lou, tentative, staying back, says, "How do you know? He's just standing there like a dummy."

"Because I know things," Mookie says. He turns now to Lou, a sadness swelling in his eyes. "I've known some things all along."

Lou shakes his head as if refusing to hear. His soulless face twists in anguish, tears gather in his eyes. "So that's it?" he says. His voice is choked, desperate. "To hell with me now, huh?"

"I'm sorry," Mookie says.

"You're sorry?" Lou shouts. "Then save *me*. You want to save everyone else, it's too late. They're dead. Save *me*."

"I can't," Mookie says. "You know."

"You lied," Lou says, shaking his head, backing away. "You were lying all along."

"Forgive me," Mookie says.

Lou wipes his eyes. "No." His hand slips into his jacket, then reappears clenched to his black pistol. He levels it at Mookie, the breast of Mookie's too-big jacket now stained with blood. "I hope you go to Hell. I hope you go *there*."

"Forgive," Mookie says. "Before it's too late."

Lou raises the gun to Mookie, whose head lilts forward like a penitent in sudden prayer. When the charcoal mat of his hair flips up, Abe's mind thinks *toupee,* but a deeper voice speaks within him, and Mookie's body slumps to the ground, his jaw popping against the cement. His dying eyes find Abe's as blood pools sickly at his cheek.

To pay.

Lou instantly falls, sobbing, onto Mookie's lifeless body. He presses his face into Mookie's back, rubs his cheek against him. Blood from the hole in Lou's shoulder electrifies the white fabric of Mookie's shirt. Lou looks up at Abe with all the evil of the world raging out from his hateful orphan's eyes. He points his still smoking gun at Abe, so that he can see into the barrel. "What am *I* supposed to do now?" he cries. "What about *me?*"

When Abe opens his mouth to offer Lou the small solace that Mookie was lost to him long ago, pictures instead of words rush from his lips. Ancient images flicker happily in the dusty light, charging the air with life. Abe's heart, so long an empty vessel, fills anew with a vast language he's always known but never felt, harmonies of sound and image, meaning compressed, time collapsed, a new measure of understanding. As movies must have been to his father when he arrived in America all those years ago. Yes. Pictures. Visions!

But Lou, unseeing, cries out once more. "Mookie!" he calls, whimpering now. "Where will I go?"

Abe reaches out to direct the man's evil, misguided attention upward to the flickering images of black and white at play on the dark ceiling — the cigarette smoke and the orchestra, the harsh, knowing spotlight, the man in the white tuxedo with sharply creased pants and the selfish, satisfied smile. But as Abe raises his arm, a *crash* rips from Lou's gun and bites into his cheek. Abe's body folds to the floor as the sky is thrown open, filled now with the man who turns on a powder white heel and sashays into the warm California light. Abe, unthinking before such beauty, asks no questions. He just rises from the floor and follows.